KATIE B. WRIGHT

Author's Note

Bella Rosa is a dual POV contemporary romance and the
first complete stand alone in The Eden Valley Series. This
book contains adult language and sexual content. Char-
acters discuss the death of a parent, past trauma, and sub-
stance abuse, however they occur off the page.

Book Cover by LorissaPadillaDesigns

Copy Editing and Proofreading by Kristen Hamilton at Kristen's Red Pen

Paperback ISBN: 979-8-9875891-1-3

Ebook ISBN: 979-8-9875891-0-6

First edition 2023

BELLA ROSA PLAYLIST

Heaven - Calum Scott

Falling Like The Stars - James Arthur

Symphony - Clean Bandit

Fred De Palma - Una volta ancora (feat. Ana Mena)

Waiting For Love – Avicii

You Are The Reason (Duet Version) – Calum Scott

The Phantom Of The Opera - Andrew Lloyd-Webber

A Thousand Miles – Vanessa Carlton

Ghost – Justin Bieber

Rhythm Inside – Calum Scott

Impossible – James Arthur

To my love. Here's to our forever.

Contents

1

A PLACE OF NEW BEGINNINGS

Rosalie

THE SUNSHINE IS DIFFERENT here. The people are too. They both have something in common. They're free.

At least that's the way I would describe it. That's the only explanation I can think of as to why everything feels so different since my plane landed a few hours ago.

I feel like I can breathe again.

Maybe it's because I'm in Europe for the first time since I was fourteen, or maybe it's because this feels like a dream come true. I can't be sure. All I know is I'm here and I'm ready for my adventure.

Three weeks. That's how long I have in Italy, in Eden Valley to be exact, to write the article that will finally get me my dream job.

When my boss Susan Williams, the editor and chief of Foodie magazine, told me about this opportunity, I thought it was a cruel joke. I'm finally being considered for a staff writer position after four years working as an editor.

I spend my days proofreading, fact checking, and editing photos for the staff writers at Foodie. I'm so tired of reading all about my colleagues' adventures. I'm glad I finally get to document my own adventure. I have the opportunity to show my writing and my own photography.

The prompt for my article is clear: *Go to the up-and-coming food destination of Italy's famous Eden Valley. Write an article talking about my favorite restaurants I eat at while on my trip. Submit the article for review at the end of my trip.*

This should be easy. I get to spend three weeks in southern Italy. I'll be two hours south of the Amalfi Coast, surrounded by beautiful rolling hills and vineyards. Sounds like the perfect place to take in the restaurant scene.

If I impress Susan and her team, I get to come back to New York to my dream job. Rosalie Mae Auclair, Staff Writer and Photographer for Foodie Magazine has a really nice ring to it if I do say so myself.

If I don't impress them, I guess I'll have to keep waitressing on the side to supplement income. Oh goodie. Being an editor doesn't cut it for the cost of living in New York and my student loan payments.

Being a twenty-six year old with two jobs doesn't always go over well at Christmas dinner as you can imagine. I've learned to ignore the snide comments from aunts and uncles I only see twice a year. That's two times too many in my opinion. Let's not talk about the constant stream of worry I get through texts from my mother.

I know I want a successful writing career and my own apartment in Manhattan that's bigger than a closet. I want free range to write about food that can change someone's life all while still being able to afford to put food on my own table.

It's why I love food so much. It's an essential part of life, but it can be made extraordinary. It can be a means of celebration, a tradition, or a vessel that holds memories. The last reason is why I love it so much.

When I think of my father, I think of food. I think of the way we used to go to new restaurants together, and the way he would always get the weirdest dish on the menu just so I could try it. He said he would sacrifice and get the weird dish so I wouldn't have to. That way if neither of us liked it we could share my food.

I feel like I'm keeping his memory alive somehow by writing about my favorite food destinations. So far those destinations have only been in New York, but now I get to experience an entirely new side of food in a place I have always dreamed about.

I push my hair out of my face and take a look around the beautiful cafe that I've turned into my sanctuary while

I wait for my train. It's been a rough eight hours to be honest. Jet lag is not going to be my friend.

But as I sit here and take in the hustle and bustle of Naples, Italy, I can't help but wonder how I got here.

A small town girl from Illinois doesn't get opportunities like this. Most positions at prestigious magazines are filled internally or through major connections. After moving to the Big Apple for college to pursue my writing degree, I fell in love with the city. All the noise allowed me to fade into the background and finally focus on myself, my love for writing, and photography. It also allowed me to stand on my own for once.

I got a lucky break when my application was accepted for assistant editor in the travel department. That may sound glamorous, but the job mostly consists of editing for grammar and not stepping foot outside of the United States.

I've been trying for this promotion for two years now. I didn't go to a prestigious school, so I'm not in the inner circle like so many of my coworkers. I often get beat out for promotions and the best assignments. I've been taking freelance jobs here and there to improve my skills and portfolio. I guess that hard work has finally paid off!

I'm not sure what snaps me out of my thoughts. It could be that I'm currently melting from the extreme heat or the nice older man sitting next to me who is trying to hand me my train ticket that I hadn't realized I had dropped beside my table. Maybe I shouldn't still be wearing my sweater from the plane and maybe I should have gone with the electronic ticket instead of one so easy to misplace. Oh well.

He holds my ticket out to me and says, "You dropped this, miss." His Italian accent is so thick I almost can't understand him.

Oh my gosh, he is the cutest old man I've ever seen. I don't know how I didn't see him sitting there before. He's kind of got the stereotypical Italian grandpa look to him. Even though he is sitting down I can tell he is on the shorter side. He has on one of those traditional gray flat caps and a suit jacket that doesn't quite match his dress pants. He is also rocking a button up shirt, bowtie, and a cane. If he was from my hometown I bet his name would be Gus.

"I see you're off to Azzurro. My daughter and her husband live there with my granddaughter. Why are you heading that way?"

I then proceed to tell him all about the new opportunity at Foodie, and just like any good grandpa, he listens intently. I wonder if my dad would have been like him. I realize I've trailed off, the memory of my dad causing my heart to ache. So I recover and conclude with, "I just don't know if I can give them what they are looking for. They have impossibly high standards and I'm not a part of the 'in' crowd. I'm just nervous that if I don't get this job I may never get another opportunity like this. This is my dream."

Wow. I don't think I've ever admitted that to anyone. I'm not entirely sure if I've ever even admitted that to myself. Unaware of my internal crisis, he gives me a light smile.

He looks at me like he knows something I don't, and says, "Don't worry. Our hearts are like a compass. They have a way of pointing us in the right direction. When you feel that pull, you'll know what you should do."

I'm not sure how that makes any sense, but he seems so confident that I can't bring myself to question him. He pushes his sleeve up enough to look down at a watch that looks like it has been worn for years.

"It looks like it's time for me to move on." He reaches over and places his wrinkled hand on mine. "Let me be the first to welcome you to the Eden Valley. A place of new beginnings. Thank you for sitting with me today."

He then reaches over to grab his cane, and with a tip of his hat he starts off in the opposite direction of the train station that's across the street.

That was such an odd encounter, but I somehow already know I'll never be able to forget it. Or him for that matter.

I didn't even get his real name. That's okay. He'll always be Gus to me.

It's then I realize I have been sitting here for far too long. If I don't leave now I'll miss my train. I fire off a text to my mother letting her know I'm about to board my train before I stand and adjust my crossbody bag.

I somehow manage to gather my mountain of belongings without causing any major catastrophes. I take one last rushed bite of my pastry and get moving. My feet are already killing me from my booties that were also a mistake in this weather, and I can barely hold my head up from exhaustion. Hopefully I can make it to the train platform without any major issues.

Matteo

Damn, this food is horrible. Cold pasta with lukewarm sauce? Not my cup of tea. I don't care if it's free. No one should be allowed to serve this shit to anyone. I guess I should just be thankful Luca is letting me sit in the employee lounge while I wait for my train.

"Earth to Matteo," Luca says while snapping his fingers in my face. I must have forgotten to act like I was paying attention.

"Sorry man. What were you saying?" I'm pretty sure he was talking about the new girl he's been seeing.

"Can't you catch a later train tonight? Mia wants you to come on a double date with us. We are planning on going to see that new movie after we grab some dinner. I think you'd hit it off with her friend Emilia."

I would rather eat gelato with soy sauce on it than go on this double date. "Nah man. I've got to get back to help at the restaurant tonight. Besides, you know I don't have time to date. I barely have time to sleep. I've got enough going on. Plus, I'm going to talk to my dad again about opening that new restaurant I've been telling you about. That'll take up even more of my time. I've got to stay focused if I want to keep expanding the business."

Plus I don't want to. He doesn't have to know that though. I've met Mia once. She was way too bubbly and energetic for me. I'm sure her friend wouldn't be any different. She needs to learn that sometimes people don't want to talk the entire time they're at dinner.

"Alright. Maybe next time. Have you made any progress getting your dad to agree to the new restaurant and your marketing plan?"

"Not really. He doesn't know why we need to expand and he doesn't understand social media. You know how he is. Never wanting to move forward with anything." Story of my life. I could never get him to agree to anything out of his comfort zone when I was growing up.

An annoying clicking sound I hear from the hallway drags me out of my childhood memories long enough to realize what time it is. Shit. I'll miss my train if I don't leave now. I gather my leather briefcase from the chair beside me, and start heading for the door. There's that clicking sound again. "Better head out or I'll miss my train."

"Well just know the invite still stands. I can't wait for us to take Mia and Emilia out together. It'll be a blast."

I doubt it.

2

TALL DARK AND DREAMY

Rosalie

I'M NOT LOST. DEFINITELY not lost and most definitely not running late. Just... uh... can't seem to find my train platform. That's all.

It must be around here somewhere. Surely train stations can't possibly be this different from those in New York.

Maybe I shouldn't have listened to the lady at the information desk who told me about this short cut.

I just need to find one of those light up boards with a map on it. Maybe then I can figure out where platform twenty-three is located in the absolutely huge train station that was very deceptive from outside.

I'm pretty sure I just passed the employee break room .

I somehow can hear muffled voices in the break room over the loud clicking of my bootie's short but practical heels that are even warmer now that I've been running around this train station for twenty minutes.

Maybe I should go in there and see if anyone can help me out real quick.

I circle back around to find the door with the break room sign on it.

Now I just need to figure out how to get the door open when my arms are full. I needed my camera bag for my assignment, but I wasn't going to leave home for three weeks without my faithful pillow I've had since I was two. My train ticket and sunglasses are also causing problems.

I proceed to let go of my very large and very overweight rolling suitcase and prop it on the wall to support my soon to be full arm. I stick my train ticket under my arm and position my sunglasses on the top of my head. Now I can transition my pillow and camera bag to the same arm, I'm kind of regretting lugging all of my very necessary possessions halfway across the world.

Just as I manage to get everything balanced and I'm as confident as I can possibly be to let go of my precious camera gear and reach out to open the door to the break room, the door swings open quickly.

I hear someone say something, but I'm too busy letting out the most unladylike squeak I've ever heard as I drop everything and start to fall backwards toward the very hard and dirty tile floor.

I'm sure I look like a scared bird with the way my arms are flapping as I try to regain my balance.

Before my body can hit the ground in a fall that would surely send me to the ER, or whatever the Italian equivalent of that is, very strong hands grab me by the upper arms and pull me into an equally strong chest.

Now that I'm not falling I realize those strong hands and chest belong to the most beautiful man I've ever seen.

Well, what I can see of him anyway. I am, in fact, pressed so close to him all I can see is the dark stubble on his chin and the sexiest smirk on his lips I've ever seen. And his smell. Oh my gosh he smells like leather and sandalwood.

Then I realize I'm clutching to his shirt with my left hand and his very nice upper arm with the other.

That means I'm not holding any of my very expensive camera gear that cost me six months worth of saving my tips.

I turn my gaze away from mystery man number one currently holding me to find an equally as beautiful, but not as captivating, man holding all my things easily in one hand.

How he's doing that, I have no idea. I'm just thankful my camera isn't in many pieces on the floor. I kind of cheaped out on the camera bag so I could get a new lens for this trip.

"Sorry about that. We didn't mean to scare you. I did manage to grab this bag before it hit the ground. It looked pretty important"

Mystery man number two has a thick Italian accent that is mouth watering. He gestures to my camera bag while barely containing a smile, his very cute dimple on full display.

"Oh, thank you," I manage to say through the noise of the erratic beating of my heart that is currently taking over my brain. I can't tell if it's from the almost fall or mystery man number one that's still holding me like I'm a trophy he just won at the state fair for best apple pie. I'll overanalyze that later. I turn my gaze back to mystery man number one and give him a small smile.

Nothing says please let go of me so I can make sure my camera is okay, and please don't ever let me go like a small smile that I'm sure doesn't look creepy at all. I'll blame the weirdness on the fact I almost just face planted in front of strangers. Seems like as good of an excuse as any.

Mystery man number one must realize he has been holding me far too long to be considered polite in our current situation. He makes sure I'm stabilized and lets go taking a few steps back.

I'm pretty sure he took all the breath from my lungs with him. I wish he would give it back.

Mystery man number two proceeds to hand my stuff back to me all while keeping a grin firmly on his face. He is tall, although not quite as tall as mystery man number one. "I'm Luca, by the way. Here's your stuff back."

He's still over six feet though, only just. He has lighter hair and is a bit broader in the shoulders than his friend. At least I'm assuming they're friends. Coworkers? He does seem to be the only one of the two wearing a station uniform. Doesn't matter.

I take my stuff back with a grateful smile.

"I'm Rosalie. Thanks for all your help. It would have ruined my trip if I had fallen and gotten hurt," I manage to get that out even though tall, dark, and dreamy over there still hasn't returned the air to my lungs.

I make the mistake of making eye contact with him. Big mistake. Huge in fact. He has the most beautiful blue eyes. Like sapphires. His dark eyebrows are drawn together and he has his hands in his pockets now.

Luca shifts his weight to his other foot as the awkwardness of the two of us staring at each other too long settles in.

"This is my very rude friend Matteo. He isn't normally so tongue-tied like this. You're from the States right? What are you doing in Naples?"

That must have really gotten Matteo to come back to life.

He is suddenly walking quickly in the direction I previously came from. Like a moth drawn to a flame I race after him.

Why I go after the guy who clearly doesn't want to talk to me, I have no idea. Luca would have been the much better option to ask for help.

"Hey! Wait up! I need some help. I got lost on my way to platform twenty-three and I can't seem to find my way to any landmarks. Can you help me at least find my way back to the main hall of the station? Or better yet, help me catch my train to Azzurro?"

It's Luca who answers instead of Matteo.

"Sure! Matteo would love to take you. In fact, that's the train he is rushing to catch as well."

Matteo never stops walking or even looks back to see the confusion on my face.

Whatever. As long as I make it to my train on time, I don't care.

I just realized I forgot to get my rolling suitcase. When I stop and turn around to get it I'm greeted by a very knowing smile on Luca's face, and my rolling suitcase being pulled behind him.

He passes it to me, but I struggle to get a good grip on it because of everything else I'm carrying.

Matteo surprises me by reaching around me and grabbing the handle instead. He barely even slows down.

"Keep up. We don't want to be late and miss the train. The next one doesn't run for hours."

Two things. One: his Italian accent isn't nearly as thick as Luca's. Two: how in the world is he so graceful with his movements?

Okay, three things. His voice is magical. I'm pretty sure I could listen to him read The Declaration of Independence and wouldn't be bored. Stop thinking about his movements and voice Rosalie and get to your train. You can daydream later.

"I'll let Mia and Emilia know you won't be able to make it, Matteo! See you later, Rosalie!" Luca suddenly belts from where he's standing. I toss a thank you and a wave over my shoulder and I hurry after Matteo.

"At least let me buy you a coffee when we get to Azzurro as thank you for all this trouble," I say through labored breaths. Man, I really need to work out more. A snort, followed by a, "No. I don't drink coffee. Just keep up.", is all I get. A snort. The man snorted. What is up with that? And how did he make that sound sexy. It must be the jet lag. Also, who doesn't drink coffee?

There are vendors and artists all along the edges of the station. I would love to stop and look, but Drill Sergeant up there won't even slow down for my much smaller legs. I have to walk twice as fast just to keep up. He has no trouble making a path through the crowd. His intimidating glare is working to our advantage.

This does give me plenty of time to admire the man though. Dark hair, but lighter than the scruff on his face. It's clear he's out in the sun a lot. The natural highlights are a dead give away, but also his beautiful olive skin. He's not overly muscular, but it's obvious he takes care of his body. He has on the perfect outfit that screams 'I don't even have to try to look this good.' Dark jeans, a dark blue t-shirt that fits him like a glove, brown shoes, and sunglasses hanging from the collar of his shirt. Why is it men can just wake up looking this attractive? It's really a crime.

His perfectly imperfect hair is shorter on the sides and longer on top, and is begging to be touched. I wonder what it would feel like to run my fingers through it. Where did that thought come from? I am losing my mind.

I can't think that about someone I just met. Especially someone as rude to me as Matteo whatever his last name is. I don't care how gorgeous he is. A girl has standards.

We finally make it to our platform after bobbing and weaving through hundreds of people, and I come to the conclusion I never would have found the platform on my own, let alone carved a path through the crowd like he did. I definitely got my steps in today and it's only 1:26 p.m. My train leaves in four minutes.

Matteo stops abruptly enough to cause me to slam the left side of my body into his solid back. He quickly hands my bag off to the attendant.

He gestures to one of the last train cars.

"There's your train." It's all I get before I see his retreating form heading to the front of the train. I will probably never see him again. Fighting a wave of disappointment, I climb on the train to find my seat.

This trip is already off to a very interesting start.

3

ALL ROSES HAVE THORNS

Matteo

SHIT. I CAN BASICALLY feel her gaze boring a hole in the back of my head as I stalk away from the most beautiful woman I've ever seen.

Why couldn't I pry my hands off her after I almost caused her to fall by opening the door in a rush? I have no idea. I wish I did. I've never acted like such a fool—a love struck fool. I fully expect a text from Luca any moment now telling me as such.

He's the reason I had to take her to the train instead of him doing his own damn job. I shouldn't need to babysit her. He was going to walk with me to the train anyway.

Maybe if I just get to my seat and catch up on some work it'll take my mind off the dark haired five foot something beauty I specifically placed four cars back. Hopefully she stays there. I will most definitely not be making the same mistake my father made. An American. Why did she have to be an American?

It doesn't matter. I don't have time to worry about a relationship anyway. I don't need any distractions. I have far too much work on my plate with the ten year anniversary of the restaurant coming up. No use in putting the effort into someone who isn't likely to stick around. My father learned that lesson the hard way. And I refuse to repeat his mistake.

Life was great living in St. Petersburg, Florida before everything went to hell. Before mom lost her shit and left us. I wasn't surprised. After her accident she got hooked on pain pills and then alcohol. Dad and I were no longer her priority.

At least she gave me one thing. My love and talent for cooking. It allowed me to go to the best culinary school in Europe and open my own restaurant with dad all by the age of nineteen. I'm proud of what I have accomplished in my twenty-nine years. I'll forever be thankful my dad signed me up for a cooking competition in high school. The grand prize was a scholarship to the local culinary school.

I somehow make it to my seat through the rows of crowded passengers and tourists. At least there's no way she can sit near me. This train is full as usual. She will have to take the first seat she finds which will hopefully be at least a few cars away.

My hometown of Azzurro and the Eden Valley that surrounds it are quickly becoming an international food destination. Thanks to my dad and I who spent the last fourteen years after we moved back trying to put the region on the map. There are so many amazing local chefs that have worked so hard to make Eden Valley a household name. It also helps that we have the coast, ancient ruins, and great weather. The perfect Italian vacation.

As soon as I sit down I feel my phone buzz. It takes far too long to wiggle my phone out of my pocket because the man sitting next to me has no sense of personal space. I mean, come on. This train doesn't have assigned seats, but I don't want to risk moving because I might see...her.

I'm not surprised to see Luca's name on the screen when I finally get my phone out of my pocket.

Luca: You're welcome.

Me: For what?

Luca: Giving you that wonderful opportunity after you almost screwed it up with that "I can't even remember my own name and I think I just pissed my pants" look that you had written all over your face.

Me: I did no such thing. I was just trying to get to my train. You know I don't have time for that shit. I've got a lot on my plate man.

Luca: Geez. I didn't say you had to marry the girl. I just thought she might be good company on the train that's all. Don't shit your pants.

Alright, moving on...

Me: It was good seeing you. Thanks for giving me a place to hang out while I waited on my train. I know you're not supposed to have anyone back there. Saved me from giving dirty looks to parents who can't shut their kids up in the waiting area. The free food was also a plus, even if it did suck ass.

Luca: No problem man. Have a safe trip. Tell your dad I said hi.

Me: Will do.

Fucker. He knows I don't have time for this shit. He means well though. He has been my best friend since the summer camp before first grade when I gave him a few of my apple slices because he forgot his lunch. I could have given him half my sandwich, but I can be a selfish fucker. Not really the best story of how I met my best friend, but it could be worse. I can always count on him though. He's basically like a brother to me. He took me in every summer when my parents and I would visit. We also went to school together after I moved back to Italy with my father. Every time I come to Naples to meet with our wine supplier I always stop by and see him. It's an easy two hour train ride, so I try to make the trip as often as I can.

He was in the Italian Special Forces for a while after high school. He's currently training to transfer to one of their intelligence special divisions. I'm glad I'll get to see him more, even if he is a pain in the ass sometimes.

After I tuck my phone away, I give my seat neighbor a death glare for how little he cares about personal space.

The glare usually works. He scoots back over to his side. Then I take my laptop out and put it on the folding tray on the back of the seat in front of me.

I begin to work on the schedule for the week, pay a few bills, and research photographers for a marketing campaign I'm planning so I can get the restaurant in a few local newspapers. At least the train has free Wi-Fi. I manage to get through making this week's schedule and paying the first few bills before my mind drifts back to light brown eyes, dark long lashes, and curls.

Rosalie.

She has a beautiful name. Fits her too. Her cheeks were the color of a rose when she realized how close I had been holding her when she almost fell. She fit so perfectly. Like she had been made for me.

She didn't smell like a rose though. She smelled like frosting and sunshine. No idea how I know what sunshine smells like, but she definitely smelled like it.

I still don't know what possessed me to reach out and grab her like that. Let alone pull her so close. It's like I couldn't help myself. I just had to touch her. I mean, I will always try and help someone if they are falling, but I didn't have to hold her that close or for as long as I did. The noise she made when she realized she was falling was cute, and the little o she made with her lips when I caught her was adorable.

It almost brought me to my knees. I had to stop myself from begging her to make the noise again. I am pathetic. And those legs. Damn. Wars have been fought for less. It didn't help that she had on a blue dress in the same style as so many of my fantasies. What was with that god awful pillow she was carrying?

Snap out of it Matteo. You don't want to get involved with a woman like that. Any woman really. Why am I analyzing her anyway? I don't do stuff like this. I meet a pretty woman, and we may help each other out here and there, but I never date. Ever.

Yeah, I have needs. But those needs haven't been met by someone other than my right hand in a while. It gets the job done just fine, and I get to stay focused all while not forming attachments. Win win.

Now if I can just get some more work done before we arrive in Azzurro. Some of my best thinking is done on trains, when I have a few hours where I can't be doing one thousand things at the restaurant. So I spent the next hour brainstorming marketing ideas and thinking about what my ideal restaurant would look like. When I'm finished, I stowaway my laptop and take in the scenery for the rest of the trip. I learned when we moved back to Italy that the city is not for me. I prefer the conveniences of a nice train station and quality restaurants, but I don't want to live in a huge city like Naples.

I keep being interrupted by thoughts of a woman in a blue dress. Before I know it my thoughts are consumed by Rosalie. I can't let it happen though; if we're going to open up a new restaurant soon, I have to stay focused. I have to keep my eyes on the prize, and I don't need any distractions, no matter how beautiful and dangerous they are. That's what she is. Dangerous. She doesn't seem like it now, but she'll show her true colors when I least expect it.

That's the trouble with roses. I never see their thorns until it's too late.

4

GARDEN OF EDEN

Rosalie

THE TRAIN RIDE WAS so beautiful I almost didn't have time to wander about Matteo. Almost. I'm human after all. No one could forget a man like that. I thought the coast was beautiful, but heading east through the rolling hills was breathtaking. Now that my train is pulling into the station, I need to focus my thoughts back to why I'm here. I can't afford to get distracted by a handsome stranger.

Luckily I put my laptop and notebook away before we arrived at the station. Now that the train has fully stopped, I stand to gather my things, and this time I secure my camera bag cross-body style so it's easier to carry everything else.

After stepping off the train onto the platform, I catch myself taking a quick look around to see if I can spot a certain tall, dark, and dreamy man. But no such luck. I was hoping to get one last look just so I can move on with my life. Oh well.

I've got a short walk ahead of me to the bed and breakfast where I will be staying. But first, I've got to make it out of the train station. Hopefully that journey won't be as eventful as getting to my train at the station in Naples. I follow the rest of the passengers who know where they are going. We make it to the exit easily. This train station seems much easier to navigate than the one in Naples.

As soon as I exit the building I'm greeted with the most amazing smell of fresh baked bread. So naturally, I follow the smell into a small little bakery with no sign and only four tables out front. The small glass display holds only a few different options, so naturally I get one of each. I bet my bed and breakfast host would like a little treat.

After securing the food in my bag—that is definitely at capacity now—I pull up my map app and type in the address for the gorgeous bed and breakfast I found through an article about the Eden Valley's hidden gems.

I didn't see many articles about the food scene even though that is what the region is starting to be known for. Maybe someday soon someone else will be researching Eden Valley for their travels and they will find my article.

I manage to orientate myself on the street and start to follow the directions on the map. It should be a six minute walk. Not bad. I just wish my suitcase didn't get stuck on absolutely every other crack and crevice on the road.

Authentic cobblestone roads are beautiful, but they are not the best walkway to pull a rolling suitcase on.

What should have been a six minute walk turns into a twenty minute walk. Of course I had to stop at every flower stand, artist booth, and bakery along the way. Not only to rest my poor arm from pulling my suitcase, but to admire all that the Eden Valley has to offer.

This city is so full of life. At this point, I'm pretty sure my pillow is permanently glued to my arm from my sweat due to the blistering heat. Though, all the locals are in long pants and seem to not even be breaking a sweat. I guess I've gotten too used to New York weather and being inside during midday.

I finally make it to the bed and breakfast. It has the most beautiful flowers growing on the front of the building. I've already spotted a coffee shop across the street that I will definitely be going to later. I make my way through the front door to the reception desk. This place seems to be deserted. I don't hear or see anyone.

There's a lot of natural light coming in through the glass door which allows me to really take a good look around. Dark wooden floors span the length of the modest entry way. I can just make out the stairs to the left. They are hidden away behind a partial wall that seems to separate the entry and the dining room.

There are old photographs along the light tan walls. A large wooden desk serves as a reception area. I let down the handle for my suitcase and then balance my pillow and camera bag on top of it. I'm so thankful for the relief of empty arms and to be out of the heat that I don't hear the footsteps of the little old lady until she is right behind me. The beautiful antique rug must have muffled her footsteps. I swear I jump ten feet in the air when I finally realize she is there. It is apparently very entertaining because she chuckles and resituates her glasses on her face.

"My you are a jumpy one, now aren't you?" She says through a friendly smile that immediately puts me at ease. She's around five feet tall with short brown hair that has a few white streaks in the front.

"You must be Rosalie. Welcome to the Eden Valley. I've got your room all ready for you. No smoking and no loud music past ten. I've got to get my beauty sleep, you know. Breakfast is at nine and dinner is at six. You don't have to attend either, but you're always welcome at my table. Now, let me show you to your room."

I like it here already. I gather my things and follow after her. "Thank you, Miss...?"

"Oh, sorry dear. You can call me Alda."

"Thank you, Alda. Do you think you could tell me about a few good restaurants around here? I'm here to

write about all the different restaurants in the Eden Valley."
I'm hopeful she will give me a list that will make my job
a lot easier. The less time I have to spend researching, the
more time I will have to actually try the new food and
write.

She strokes the long gold pendant around her neck while
we walk up the stairs. She doesn't answer right away.

We make it to the landing and continue walking down a
long hallway of what seems to be all the guest rooms. The
hallway is illuminated by a large window at the end where
a small chair and side table sit, the open window causing
the curtains to sway in the small space.

I am just beginning to wonder if she heard me when
she finally answers. "I'll get my daughter to help you. She
keeps up with all that stuff much more than I do. She owns
the Polpo Café across the street. She serves some very nice
lunches, pastries, and drinks." I can tell just how proud she
is of her daughter. So much so that it brings a smile to my
face.

"Oh thank you so much! That would be wonderful.
Maybe I can go over in the morning to talk to her. When
does she open?" I hope she can hear just how excited and
thankful I am.

"She opens at eight. You can go then. She doesn't get her
morning rush until around nine. Ah, here we are, dear.

Please let me know if you need anything. Towels are under the sink." She opens the door to my home for the next three weeks. I shuffle into the picturesque room and take in the space.

"Can I ask you something?"

She shifts some keys around in her pocket. "Of course."

I turn so I'm facing her. "What's the story behind the Eden Valley? I did so much research before coming here, but I couldn't find the reason behind the nickname."

She walks over to a photograph on the wall of the countryside. "This area is situated in between two mountain ranges. A few hundred years ago three brothers left home and traveled south to the area we are in now. No one knows where they came from. They left in search of better opportunities and happiness. They fell in love with the lush green landscape and the rolling hills. Within the first year, all three were married and owned successful businesses. They contributed their success to this area of Italy. They said it was like living in the Garden of Eden, so when word traveled back home of their success the locals started referring to it as the Eden Valley."

I look out the window at the beautiful landscape. The view of the city with the rolling hills in the background is breathtaking. "I can see why the brothers were so impressed."

She pats me on the shoulder as she walks by. "Enjoy your stay."

Alda leaves, shutting the door behind her, and I begin exploring. It doesn't take long because the room isn't huge, but it does have a private bathroom. I really didn't know what to expect when I booked a bed and breakfast on this side of town. From what I could tell online, this area is mostly frequented by locals instead of tourists.

The room is painted a light blue color with the same dark wood flooring from downstairs. In the right corner of the room there is a twin bed with a white quilt. A small antique writing desk and chair are under the open window in the center of the wall directly ahead. With similar light-weight curtains to the hallway, the summer breeze coming in is causing them to sway. Hopefully the open window won't let any bugs in.

The door to the bathroom and the small wardrobe are on the left wall. There are photographs very similar to the ones in the entryway scattered all around the room.

I start unpacking right away. I place my beloved pillow on the bed and open my suitcase. I would love to explore some before it gets too dark outside, but by the time I get unpacked it will probably be close to dinner time.

I should probably eat with Alda tonight. I doubt I'll have time to research any restaurants before dinner. That can wait until after. Maybe I can create a small list of places I would like to go before I meet Alda's daughter tomorrow. That way she can add to my list and let me know if I'm on the right track. I wish I had more time to research before I came. This was kind of a last minute trip, so I focused most of my time on my accommodations.

After a quiet dinner with Alda and a few other guests who didn't speak any English, I head back up to my room to wash away the grime of a travel day. I also found out the bed and breakfast seemed empty earlier because most of the guests were out exploring. There are currently no vacancies.

After I make it into the shower, which is surprisingly modern, I start to think back about my first day in Italy. It seems like it's been three or four days wrapped up in one. My mind immediately goes to Matteo just like it did while I was unpacking and while I was eating dinner. I can't seem to get him off my mind. The way he held me. His smell. I shouldn't think of him. I'll never see him again. He was so rude, and he has a girlfriend. However, the throbbing between my legs betrays my thoughts. Traitor.

I turn the water temperature as cold as I can stand it to try and put out the fire Matteo caused from one touch. I'm pitiful.

I quickly get through my shower and dry off. I need to stay focused and do some research before bed. The first day of the journey to my dream job starts tomorrow. I can't lose focus, no matter how much my body may want me to. That's all this is. A simple reaction to him holding me that way. It's been far too long, and my body just didn't know how to respond in a normal way. That's it. That's all this is.

Whatever you need to keep telling yourself, Rosalie.

5

POLPO CAFÉ

Rosalie

I wake up the next morning to my alarm blaring on my phone, and roll over and groan. I reach over to turn the annoying thing off so I can make my way out of bed. My first night here was wonderful, even though I still feel like I could sleep for the rest of the day. I'm normally an early riser, but seven-thirty in the morning doesn't hit the same when paired with jet lag.

After getting ready for the day, in much more weather appropriate clothing I might add, I make my way down the stairs with my camera bag. I've got the list of restaurants I found during my research last night tucked in the back pocket of my jean shorts. I find Alda putting a few dishes on the dining room table. She turns my way with a warm smile. "Good morning! I hope you slept well and found the room to your liking."

"It was wonderful. Thank you. I was thinking about going on over to talk to your daughter." I say hoping she hasn't changed her mind about agreeing to help me with my restaurant search.

"I spoke with her last night after dinner. She is so excited to meet you."

"Wonderful! I'll go ahead and head over now. Thanks again for all your help." I start toward the door as I hear a few other guests making their way down the stairs.

As soon as I open the door I'm stopped in my tracks. The natural lighting this morning is just perfect for photographs. I stop and take in the beauty of the street for a moment. It's not too busy yet, but I know this is a street the locals often use instead of just the tourists. My research is proving to be correct so far.

There are two mothers walking together with their children riding scooters in front of them. One older man is walking with a coffee in hand and the morning newspaper under his arm. A middle aged man is walking quickly with a briefcase in one hand, and a lunch box in the other.

After snapping a quick photo of the front of the bed and breakfast in the morning sun, I make my way across the street to the bakery. The buildings on this street all seem original on the outside, but quite modern on the inside. They've not lost their Italian flare though. The beautiful bakery has four small two-seater tables out front, a sign above the door with Polpo Café written in script, and a standing sign on the sidewalk with handwritten daily specials.

I step through the open glass door, and am greeted by the wonderful smell of freshly baked pastries. I take a look around while making my way to the counter. Shades of white, peach, and pink are artfully placed on the walls and throughout the decorations of the open concept bakery. The young woman behind the counter looks like she was born to be in this space. She fits in with the decorations perfectly. She seems to be huffing and puffing over something behind the counter that I can't see.

She has long strawberry blond hair that's currently pulled up in a messy ponytail, with a few stray pieces around the edges of her face. She seems to be around my age.

She whirls around quickly when she hears me. A look of shock is written all over her beautiful face. She has a light dusting a freckles across her nose, and striking green eyes.

"Oh, hello. Welcome to Polpo Café. So sorry, but it looks like I won't be serving any cannolis this morning. It looks like I've just broken my mixer." She wipes her hands on her apron as she walks toward the register. "Is there anything else I can get for you? Everything in the display case was freshly baked this morning."

I take a quick scan of the display case before saying, "I'm actually staying with Alda across the street. She said I could come over and talk to her daughter about local restaurants."

With a beaming smile she says, "Oh yes! Mamma called me last night. You must be Rosalie. I'm Julianna, Alda's daughter. You can call me Juli if you'd like. I'm so glad you're here! Please come sit." She starts to move over to one of the five small tables while gesturing to one of its chairs. "I am so passionate about the local restaurants around here. So many chain restaurants have moved in over the last few years because of how popular the city has gotten. It's so difficult to promote local businesses now."

I take a seat and reach into my back pocket to pull out my list. "That's why I'm here! I would love to write an article featuring local restaurants in the Eden Valley. Here's what I have come up with so far." I hand her the list I made last night hoping I don't seem like a fool.

It was much harder than I thought to find local restaurants online. "I was hoping you could tell me if I was on the right track." I lay my hands in my lap and try not to fidget while I wait for her to read over the list of eight restaurants that seemed local.

She takes a pen from a pocket on her apron, and starts to mark out items on the list. "These are definitely not worth your time." She marks a question mark next to a few. "These are okay, but not special. This one is wonderful." Pointing to one she just marked with a star. "You must try their mushroom risotto." She makes a few notes then starts writing at the bottom of the list. "This is one of my favorite local restaurants. You should try this one as soon as you can." She marks that one with two stars.

After we talk a few more minutes about the list she has created, she slides the paper back to me. I take a photo of it on my phone for good measure, and stick it back in my pocket. "Thank you so much. You've really been such a big help already. Do you think I could try a few pastries, and take a lunch sandwich to go?"

We sit for a while and she tells me stories about growing up in Italy while I eat. I make sure and snap pictures of all the cute and delicious pastries she hands me. I manage to say through a mouth full of food, "So you mean to tell me, you hiked all forty miles, alone? Are you crazy! Aren't you afraid of bears?"

She rolls her eyes and gestures wildly with her hands. "I had bear spray. I was completely safe. I almost ran out of food though. You don't realize how hungry you get on a trip like that." We keep talking for the next few hours. She gets up every so often to tend to customers. I tell her all about Foodie magazine and about my encounter at the train station with the mystery man.

She makes a disbelieving noise and pats me on the arm in solidarity. "He sounds like a dick. Hopefully you'll never have to see him again."

"His friend was nice." I shake my head and try to shift my concentration to the pattern on the table. I need something else to focus on so I don't show how much he bothers me. I have no idea why. It's not like I actually know the man. "It doesn't matter though. I'll never see him again."

She nods her head in agreement while I stand from my chair and dust the crumbs from my lap. It's already after lunch time. I didn't realize how long we had been chatting. "I've got to get going. Thank you so much for all your help, the wonderful food, and for the company. I really had a lot of fun. Will you be at your grandmother's for dinner any night this week?"

She pulls out her phone while she stands. "Looks like I'll have a free evening on Thursday. I'll come over then and we can catch up and see if you need any more recommendations!"

As I walk out the door I send a wave over my shoulder. "Sounds perfect!"

As soon as I get back to my room I dig my laptop out of my bag and start to look up the restaurants on my new list. Pretty soon I realize over half of them aren't within walking distance and it looks like there aren't any train stations near them either. Maybe I could take the bus, or a taxi. I didn't realize this city wasn't really built for walking.

Sounds like a later problem to me, because I'm going to the one Julianna marked with two stars tonight. It's within walking distance, and the menu I managed to find online looks amazing. They don't have a website though. I couldn't even find a phone number. Dated much?

Now I just need to find an outfit for dinner tonight. Sounds like the perfect time to wear my favorite dress since this is one of Julianna's favorite places in the city. You can't go wrong with a little black dress. Especially when going somewhere named Moretti's.

6

Enjoy Life While You Can

Matteo

A FULL HOUSE. JUST the way I like it. I make my way through the crowded restaurant to the kitchen. I tip my head at my manager. "How are we doing tonight? Any issues I should know about?"

He runs his fingers through his hair and lets out a deep breath. "We're still having some issues with the deliveries. We can talk about it later when we aren't as busy. I'm getting my ass kicked tonight."

I nod my head and make my way to the back of the busy kitchen and through the door that leads to my closet of an office. I know I can count on my staff to tell me the truth. I hired the best of the best for that reason. I sit down at my small dark wooden desk and drag a hand through my hair and down my face. It's been a long night, and it's not even halfway over.

Nothing has gone wrong exactly. I'm just worked up about the talk I'm about to have with my father about my plans for the next restaurant. I want to run it differently than this one. More modern. More innovative.

I hear my father's distinct footsteps and the creak of his office door opening and closing next door. I adjust my tie as I stand. It's game time. I take a deep breath as I push open my door and walk the few feet over to his office. I stare at the plaque on the door that reads Lorenzo Moretti for a moment before I knock. The delay in his answer seems like an eternity.

"Come in." I hear through the solid wood door that I've walked through more times than I can count. This time seems different though.

I open the door to the office my father has had for the last ten years. The only thing that has changed are the pictures in the frames on the walls. His office is bigger than mine, but feels smaller because it's so cluttered. Picture frames filled with memories of the two of us and piles of papers line the walls and his desk. He says he works best this way. Who am I to judge, even though it would drive me insane. The clutter makes my left eye twitch every time I come in here.

"Come in. Come in. I just got off the phone with our financial advisor, James. He is very pleased with the growth of the last quarter."

"I'm sure Josh was very pleased. That's actually what I wanted to talk to you about." I put emphasis on the man's real name hoping my father will finally learn it after all these years. He is horrible with names. Never forgets a face though. My father sits back in his chair and motions for me to take a seat in the only other chair in the room. His desk is facing a wall because the space is so small. He swivels around so he is fully facing me. "I would like to have a conversation about opening another location, if you have time to listen to some of my ideas right now."

He doesn't look thrilled but he nods.

I clear my throat and begin the speech I practiced in the shower this morning. "Profits would be higher if we opened another location that was more modernized and appealed to a younger crowd. We could maintain a similar feel, but modernize it a bit so the younger crowd wants to come visit. We need to build an online presence and show the tourists that they can eat at a local restaurant and not just the faster-paced tourist traps. I have a few ideas on new menu items and possible locations. We've saved up enough money to make it happen. We're missing out on so many customers because we don't appeal to the tourists and younger crowd." When I finish, I sit back in my chair and I wait for his response.

I knew I needed to lead into this slowly. My father needs time to adjust to new ideas if there is any hope in him accepting them. That's why I've been dropping hints for the past few months as a lead up to this formal conversation. Hopefully that decision doesn't backfire.

He takes his glasses off and rubs his eyes. "I don't know why you are so hung up on this idea. We don't need to expand. We are doing just fine here. It's not just about profits, son." He places his glasses back on and looks at me. "I just don't want to risk losing what we have here, Matteo. We have such a good thing going, so I don't want to rock the boat and risk messing it up. I wish you would take some time off every now and then. Enjoy life while you can instead of working yourself to death like you've been doing the past few years."

"You don't have to do anything. Let me do it. I want to do it," I reply. I want to do it for you. To show you mom didn't ruin everything when she left. She didn't ruin us or the future we could have. Even though she did sell our house, and the car. She could have ruined everything because she sold it all. Just so she could buy a few more pills. But she didn't. I won't let her. I don't voice all these thoughts because he doesn't need to hear them, but they're there and the driving force behind why I want to do this so badly.

He looks at me for a moment. "I'll think about it." That's all I can ask for. We both stand at the same time. He pulls me in for a hug like I'm still a small child even though I've got four inches on him. "I'm so proud of you, son. I hope you'll always know that."

I clear my throat and pat him on the back. "Thanks, dad."

We both pull away and I make my way toward the door. I close it quietly behind me and make my way to the bar. I need to check in with our bartender to see what needs to be ordered this week. I call it a bar, but it's not a typical bar. More like a walk up counter with a few drink options and a place for people to pick up takeout orders since it's pretty close to the reception desk.

Before I can even reach the bar I hear a very loud customer complaining about something at the reception desk. What now? I don't have time for this shit tonight. I'm already behind on all my work because I was preparing for the meeting with my dad.

I round the corner and come to a dead stop. What the fuck is she doing here? Rosalie. I never thought I would see her again. And what the hell is she wearing? Those legs are peeking out through a very long slit in her dress that hugs every curve on her beautiful body. She looks even taller in the heels she's wearing. Her hair is pulled up in a low bun that shows off her slender neck.

I discreetly adjust myself in my pants, and make my way over to her. I can't help myself. I come up behind the poor hostess that seems terrified by this mesmerizing woman that I still haven't taken my eyes off of. "What seems to be the problem here?"

That's when she stops talking and freezes. She quickly composes herself and points a finger at me like I'm the one doing something wrong. "What are you doing here?"

I raise an eyebrow. "I work here."

"Can you please help me get a table?"

She sounds like it's painful to admit she needs help. Too bad I'm not going to give it to her. "No. We're full. Make a reservation and come back another night."

I start to move away, but she reaches out and grabs my arm. The electric shock that rolls though my body is enough to stop me in my tracks. What the hell was that? She comes around the hostess stand and gets within a few inches of me. She's so close I can see now she has green along the edges of her otherwise light brown eyes. Oh shit. I have no business noticing things like that.

"Please help me get a table. I'm writing an article for Foodie magazine and this is one of the only restaurants that was recommended to me within walking distance. It took me fifteen minutes to walk here, and I don't want to walk back right away in these shoes." She gestures to her shoes while continuing to rapidly fire more words I can't seem to pay attention to. I don't think I could break eye contact if there was a gun to my head, and that scares the shit out of me.

"Fine. Get her a table."

If she is really writing an article for that magazine we could use the publicity. I could use that to show my dad why we need to advertise more. Plus, I don't want her to walk back alone in the dark. Not exactly sure why I even thought about that to be honest, but here we are.

My hostess is now in full panic mode. "But sir, we're full."

I finally manage to break the spell and look away. "Give her the chef's table in the kitchen." I notice she hasn't taken her hand from my arm, and I have no intention of moving it for her.

The hostess gives me a nod as she gathers a menu and some silverware. "Right this way."

She begins walking in the direction of my private table in the kitchen. The table is normally reserved for visiting chefs or my friends. Rosalie gives my arm a quick squeeze before she lets go. The sudden loss of contact causes my eyes to meet hers again, and I'm rewarded with the most genuine smile I've ever seen. That smile causes my heart to do a weird flip flop.

She turns to walk away. Apparently I've been standing in the same spot for so long the hostess has enough time to return. She clears her throat, and gives me a strange look. "Was there anything else, sir?"

"No. That's all." I turn and head back toward my office so I don't do anything stupid like go over and ask Rosalie what her favorite color is for God knows what reason. Thankfully the chef's table is on the other end of the kitchen from my office. Small mercies.

When I get back to my office I pull my phone out of my pocket and fire off a text to Luca.

Me: I'm so screwed.

Luca: *rose emoji*

Ah shit.

7

THE PACT

Rosalie

WHY HIM? WHY MATTEO of all people? And why did he have to look so damn good tonight in his dark green button up shirt with the sleeves rolled up to his elbows? I can't believe he works here. I can still feel him watching me as I walk through the doors of the kitchen. I'm glad he can't hear how fast my heart is beating.

I rub my hand on my leg as I take my seat and thank the hostess. I can still feel his warmth on my hand and feel the shock that went through me when I touched him. I don't know why I did it. I guess I was just so desperate to not have to walk back right away, and I really wanted to eat here tonight.

The place smells and looks amazing. It's nice, but not too fancy. The red walls and dark wood flooring of the main room create such a homey feeling in the huge space. Well, huge for Italy, from what I'm gathering anyway. If more than ten tables can fit inside a building it classifies as huge it seems. I guess that's why so many restaurants choose to be outside the city. The little lights hanging from the ceiling make me feel like I'm in my own private garden.

The light gray walls, stainless steel surfaces, and tile flooring of the kitchen are a stark contrast from the main room. I can't believe I get to sit in the kitchen and watch everyone work.

I pick up my menu and order a glass of wine and an appetizer when my waiter shows up a few minutes later. He smiles and fills an empty glass that was already on the table with water. I realize too late that it's sparkling water, and almost choke before I even get to try the bread. At least no one saw me. That would have been embarrassing.

The rest of the meal goes smoothly. I get plenty of photos for my article, and make notes about my experience on my notepad I always keep in my large bag. I opted for a large purse tonight with my camera tucked safely inside instead of my full camera bag. Draws less attention this way, and it was less weight to carry on the walk over.

I'm almost positive this is the best food I've ever had. When my waiter comes back again to ask if I want dessert, I ask him to give my compliments to the chef. I will definitely be including this restaurant in my article.

Matteo

"She said what?" I can't keep the smile from my face.

"She said this was the best Italian food she's ever had. She wanted me to send her compliments to the chef. She specifically said she could feel the heart behind the food. Whatever that means."

My head waiter seems confused, but I know exactly what she means. You can tell when someone actually thinks about what they cook instead of just following the standard recipe handed down from their grandmother. There's nothing wrong with that, but if you want someone to stop and think about what makes your food different, then you have to step outside the box every now and then.

My feet are moving before I even have a say in the matter. "Sir, where are you going? We need to discuss the issue with the deliveries."

I hear him, but I don't care. I just want to know why she said what she did. I burst through the kitchen door and startle at least half a dozen people. I make my way around to her table and she lets out a little gasp when she sees how worked up I am.

"Why did you say what you said?" I'm not sure why it matters so much to me. All I know is I have to know the answer.

"What?" She asks in a low voice, looking at me like I'm crazy.

I repeat her words. "Why did you say you can feel the heart behind the food?"

A small blush creeps on her cheeks. She looks down at her hands that are clasped in her lap and smiles. Her smile is soft. Not like the one from before that made my heart do that weird thing, but it's there. "My father used to talk about how you can always tell if someone cares about what they cook. If they want to put their own stamp on it. I can tell your head chef cares a great deal. I'm sorry I made such a scene earlier. This is just such a big deal for me."

I pull out the chair across from her and sit down. "I'm the head chef." She looks at me with the cutest confused expression on her face. "I'm the owner actually. Co-owner specifically. My dad and I own the restaurant. Every night that I can I'm the acting head chef. On nights like tonight when I have admin things to do, my sous chef takes over for me."

She's still looking at me like I grew two heads.

"Are you really writing an article for Foodie magazine?" There's no way, right? That's a crazy popular magazine in the food community. I can't let myself get my hopes up about having an article with my restaurant in it.

My question about the article helps her find her words. "Yes. It's actually like a trial period for me. If all goes well they will publish my article and I'll become a full time writer and photographer for them."

Her small smile has returned, and so has mine. My restaurant could be in Foodie. That's insane. I let out a loud laugh. "That's incredible! I can't believe you're going to write about Moretti's!"

She lets out a little gasp. "You have a wonderful laugh. Oh my gosh did I say that out loud?" She slaps a hand over her mouth so fast it makes a smacking noise.

We both start laughing so hard there are tears running down our faces by the time we realize the ruckus we've made. I reach over and catch a tear that's falling down her cheek. She stops and stares at me with wide eyes, and I pull my hand back quickly. I don't know what came over me. I'm acting like a fool. I clear my throat to try and regain some composure. "How long are you here for?" I must like to torture myself.

"Three weeks." Damn. That's confirmation I shouldn't get involved. I don't think she's the type of girl that would be okay with a quick fling, so there's nothing for us.

I snag a waiter that is walking by. "Can you bring us some more wine?" I then direct my attention back to the dark haired beauty across from me. "What's your plan?"

She gets a furrow in her brow. "Excuse me?"

I lean back in my seat to give the waiter enough room to pour my wine. I hadn't realized I was leaning forward so much. "What's your plan for the rest of your stay? You have to have a plan, or you'll waste time."

She nods her head and starts digging through her massive purse. She hands me a crumpled up piece of paper that has a list of well known restaurants on it. "Right. My bed and breakfast host got her daughter to help me with a list of restaurants to check out."

I'm impressed. I pull a pen out of my pocket and start writing. "This is a good list. I know most of the owners. They would be very happy to have you come by. You'll want to make reservations for these as soon as possible. If you need help getting in, give them my name. That should secure you a good table."

She sighs and says, "That's the problem. Most of them are too far for me to walk. I'll have to drive, and I don't even have an up-to-date drivers license. I live in New York.

I only ever take the subway. Are there a lot of ride sharing options around here?"

"There are in the city, but not where some of these restaurants are." She slouches back in her seat looking defeated. Oh shit. Don't say it. Don't say it. "I could take you." Fuck.

Her face lights up as she shoots forward in her seat. "No way! Are you serious? Are you sure it's not too much trouble?"

Oh it absolutely is, but I need to make sure there's even an article for her to write if I want my restaurant to be in it. "It's no trouble." I give her a small smile that she returns tenfold. That causes another flip flop in my chest. I add a few more names to the bottom of the list. "These restaurants will be having soft openings within the next couple of weeks. A soft opening is—"

"Like a trial run."

I look up to see her watching me intently. "Yes. Like a trail run."

She smiles as she picks up her wine glass. "This is kind of my job, remember?"

I can't help but smile at her. The little firecracker. "Right. My mistake." I shift my gaze back to the paper and I make a few more notes. "These are mostly open for lunch.

You can easily walk to them though, so that shouldn't be a problem."

She suddenly breaks my concentration. "How did you get so good at this?"

I place my pen down on the table and rub my chin. "A decade in the business is bound to teach you a few tricks."

She's the one that leans forward now. Her sudden movement causes the air to shift and her delicious scent to fill my space. I feel my nostrils flare as I try to keep my composure at the sudden intrusion. I watch as she studies me. Her gaze roaming over my face. I wonder what she finds in her inspection. "That's quite impressive, Mr. Moretti."

I shake my head as I lean forward so my elbows rest on the table. "Don't call me that. That's my fathers name."

I can tell she's holding back a smile. "Just Matteo then?"

I feel my breath catch at hearing her say my name. "Just Matteo."

She places her napkin on the table and pushes her seat back. "Thank you for your help," she says as we both stand. She gathers her things and spins around to look at me. "I'm really so grateful. I know that my article will be so much better if I have a real chef there to answer my questions! I've really got to be going now. I like to write when the experience is fresh on my mind."

Right on queue one of my busboys, Enzo, comes over to clear her table and says exactly what I told him to say, "Hey boss man, this is my last table. I'll be heading out after this. Need anything else before I go?" He looks up at me like a child would when a parent tells them to say please and thank you.

Rosalie is still gathering her things. "Sure, can you take Rosalie back to where she is staying? I'd rather her not walk back in the dark."

She whips her head around to stare at me like I just told her to stand on her head and sing the happy birthday song. "Oh that's not necessary." She says it like she doesn't mean it at all.

"Oh it would be no trouble at all, miss. I'm Enzo," he answers with a smile, also just like I told him to do. He sticks his hand out to take hers. As soon as they make contact I feel all the muscles in my body go hard as stone. Interesting.

"If it's really no trouble." She inches forward with a hopeful look on her face. I knew she didn't want to walk back, and I didn't want her to walk back. I just couldn't offer to take her because that feels too much like a date. Taking the lady home after she ate a nice dinner in a nice dress like that. Too much. I did come up with this plan before I offered to take her to nice dinners pretty much every day for the next three weeks. That's business though. I'm only doing that so she will keep us in the article, after all.

"No problem at all. Just let me go get my things." He says as he picks up the last few plates off the table. He uses that opportunity to sneak a peek at her cleavage.

I grab a receipt book from a passing waiter and write my number down. I hand her the paper with my number. "Text me and we will work out the details of our little pact here."

She takes the paper and looks at it before putting it in her purse. "Pact?"

I take a step closer to her. I've got to put some expectations on this before my dick can have his own way. "This is a mutually beneficial business arrangement." She goes still at my sudden change in tone. "I take you on this grand food tour and you make sure my restaurant is in the article at the end of the three weeks. Deal?" I stick my hand out for a hand shake, but regret it the moment she touches me. There's that shock again. I'll add it to the list of things I need to talk about with my doctor.

"Deal," she says as she shakes my hand more forcefully than necessary. She picks up her bag and starts walking to the front of the restaurant. "I'll be out front," she adds, looking at Enzo. She's not put off by my coldness as she walks away with her head held high. Good girl.

Enzo tries to follow her like a lost puppy. I grab him by the collar and yank him back into the storage room. I push him up against the wall a little harder than intended.

"What the hell?" He squeaks out.

Still holding him by his shirt collar, I get up in his face. "If you so much as think about touching her, not only will you be fired, but I will set you on fire. You got me?"

He nods his head so quickly I'm afraid it will fall off.

"Good. Now get out of here." I release him and step back out into the main room. I adjust the tie around my neck as I walk to the kitchen. What came over me? I never lash out like that.

If I didn't need to get away from her so badly I would tell Enzo to screw off and I would just take her myself. I can't do that though. I have got to get away from her to clear my head.

Plus, I have to move my schedule around for the next three weeks if I'm going to be spending so much time with Rosalie.

When I get back to my office I have a text waiting for me.

Rosalie: I'll see you at 6pm tomorrow for dinner. Pick me up at my bed and breakfast. I'll send you the address.

Me: Sweet dreams, Rosa.

What the hell have I gotten myself into?

8

MYSTERY MAN

Rosalie

"NO WAY! YOU DIDN'T tell me your rude mystery man is Matteo!" Juli can't contain her excitement.

I can barely concentrate on what she's saying. I tossed and turned all night. My dreams were plagued with visions of broody eyes and sun streaked hair. I take a long drink from my coffee cup before I answer. "It didn't seem important to tell you his name."

I return my focus back to the list of restaurants in front of me to try and plan out the rest of the week. I already made reservations for tonight. I won't make a fool of myself like I did last night ever again.

"Well it was!" Juli pushes the list out of my line of vision so I'll look at her. "He's my cousin! My mom and his dad are siblings!"

"What? That's a crazy coincidence."

Juli nods as she says, "I know, right! Matteo has been through a lot, but he's such a great guy."

I look down at my now empty coffee cup and sigh. Not just about the empty cup, but about him. It took me so long to calm down after our encounter last night that I could barely sleep. Also, I'm pretty sure Enzo never even made eye contact with me on the way back to Alda's last night. He also looked like he'd seen a ghost when he picked me up in his little car out front.

Juli snaps her fingers in my face. "Have you been listening to me?" I give her a blank look, shaking my head to try to clear my thoughts. "I guess not. You really should give him a chance though. I have always wanted him to find a girl like you."

She has to be kidding. "There's no way. He was so rude at the train station, and last night he made up this whole pact thing." I do the motion for air quotes around the word pact for emphasis. "He made it very clear he wants nothing to do with me. I don't know if I want anything to do with him either."

She takes a bite of her breakfast before standing to get a refill of our coffees and completely ignores what I said. "Don't worry, you'll have a great time tonight. That restaurant is wonderful, and Matteo can be so fun after he loosens up a bit."

I'm sure she's right. I need to loosen up and enjoy this experience. I snap a few photos of the display case while

Juli finishes up at the front counter. We decided to try a bakery a few streets away this morning. It's Juli's day off, and she offered to do a little sightseeing with me. Walking around the city square and going to a few local museums are just what I need after how hectic the past few days have been.

I hear the little bell signaling the front door just opened. I feel the air shift around me. I know he's there before I even look up. I like to torture myself, apparently, because I immediately look up and make eye contact with him. He's already looking right at me. I can tell even though he still has his sunglasses on.

He's standing there looking like a model in his dark jeans and fitted black shirt. He takes his sunglasses off and runs his other hand through his hair. I follow the motion like my life depends on it.

"Oh hi there, Matteo!" Juli sing-songs from behind me. I bolt upright from my squatting position by the display case causing my sunglasses to fall off my head. I don't even have the wits about me to try and catch them. I'm too caught up in the storm that is Matteo Moretti.

He finally breaks eye contact to look over at Juli. "Hi Juli. How's the bakery doing? I'll have to come in soon to get some desserts for Luca's birthday." He smiles as he reaches out to give her a side hug.

I must be doing a horrible job at hiding my feelings because after they let go of each other Juli gives me the 'what is wrong with your face' look. I bet my face is so red it looks like I forgot sunscreen on a week long cruise in the Bahamas. Great. I can't seem to stop embarrassing myself.

I bend down to pick up my sunglasses and tuck a stray hair behind my ear. "Good morning Matteo," I say as I return to a somewhat normal standing position. As normal as one can be when they don't know what to do with their hands in an extremely awkward situation.

He gives me a full smile that almost knocks me to my knees again. I manage to stay upright, thankfully. I don't think my sunglasses would survive another fall.

He takes a step toward me and swallows me whole with one look. Suddenly I'm surrounded by leather and sandalwood. It's quickly becoming my favorite scent. He speaks so low I can barely hear. "Sleep well, Rosa?"

I unintentionally take a step toward him. "No." I breathe out.

"Me either," he says as he takes another step in my direction.

The door opening again causes us both to return to reality. We are very much in the way of the flow of traffic for the small space in the bakery. We separate, and allow the new customers to walk up to the counter. After they pass he starts towards the counter while talking over his shoulder. "See you tonight, Rosa."

Juli grabs me by the arm and pulls me through the door and I'm grateful for the fresh air. As soon as the door closes she lets go of my arm and spins around. "What the hell was that?"

She's motioning to the door we just came through and staring at me like I should know the answer to her question. I open my mouth to say I have no idea, but she keeps talking. "I almost caught fire from the heat coming off the two of you. You didn't tell me he was interested in you! Oh my gosh, he looked like he was going to mount you in the middle of the bakery, and you looked like you were going to let him. Spill!"

I take a deep breath to give myself more time to think of an explanation. Giving up I finally admit, "I have no idea. We talked some last night at dinner, but I already told you everything he said while we were eating breakfast. I'm just as confused as you are. I thought he hated me. He made it very clear last night this was only a business arrangement. Plus, I overheard him talking about his girlfriend at the train station when we met. Remember?"

We start walking in the direction of a little boutique at the end of the street. She locks arms with me to make sure we don't get separated in the sea of people. "Well all I know is, that was hot, like so hot I can't wait to hear how tonight's dinner goes. I want a play by play first thing in the morning. I've not heard about him dating anyone, so it must be a new thing. We have some similar friends because we grew up together. He was only a few years ahead of me in school."

We end up shopping and walking around for a few hours. My feet are so numb, I'm pretty sure I left them laying in the middle of the street. My mind, however, is back at the bakery with Matteo. I've been replaying our encounter all day.

We find a seat outside our lunch destination and dig into our sandwiches. I still have some of my brain working enough to remember to snap a few photos before eating. As soon as I take the first bite, I feel like a new person. I didn't realize how hungry I was.

Juli points at me with her sandwich which causes a little piece of tomato to fall to the table. "So what are you going to wear tonight?"

I take a little sip of my lemonade while I think through all the clothes I brought with me. "Maybe a white dress that's fitted on the top and flowy at the bottom. I brought some cute wedges to go with it too. That way I don't break an ankle on this cobblestone." I half heartedly kick the cobblestone for good measure.

Juli gives me a big nod and an even bigger smile. "That'll be perfect. You are going to blow his mind!"

I roll my eyes and point back at her with what's left of my sandwich. "Hey! Knock it off! Nothing is going to happen."

Now it's her turn to roll her eyes. "Whatever you say, girlfriend."

We finish eating, and head back to Alda's so I can show Juli my dress for tonight. Even Alda comes up to my room to see my outfit, and sits with us for a while. They even bring out their old photo albums.

This all feels so foreign to me. My mom and I have never done anything like this. Hell, we only see each other a few times a year. After my parents divorced when I was six, I didn't spend much time with my mom. When my dad died she reluctantly took me in. I was a disruption to her carefully constructed life. She was a lawyer, so she had plenty of money to spend on lavish vacations with her friends. So I spent a lot of time with various babysitters until I was finally old enough to stay on my own. I feel a tightness in my chest as I realize what I could have had.

Alda shakes her head while she looks at me through the mirror. "I just can't believe he would have a girlfriend. I've never known of him to date. He's such a serious boy. He seems so consumed with that restaurant of his. Are you sure you heard him correctly?"

"Luca mentioned telling two girls he couldn't make it to something."

"Ouch!"

I swat at the hair brush Juli is using in my rats nest I like to call hair. The wind was not my friend today. "Sorry!" She gives me a small smile before resuming her task. "I just want you to look perfect tonight, and let's be honest... you need some help with this mane of yours." She motions to all my hair. It's always been unruly, and I've always kept it long. It's currently down to the end of my rib cage.

"There! You're ready." Juli says while spinning me around so I can use a handheld mirror and the vanity mirror to look at the back of my hair.

"Oh don't you look lovely," Alda says as she pushes a stray hair out of my face.

It's a simple half up hair style, but it's way more than I would have been able to do. Juli used two braids to pull my hair back into a small bun. It's so beautiful I have to keep myself from touching it.

I stand from the vanity, and give her a hug. "Thank you! It is absolutely beautiful."

"Of course," Juli answers.

I add a few finishing touches to my makeup, before I put on my shoes. "How do I look?"

I do a little twirl for dramatic effect. I did my eye makeup a little darker tonight to edge it up a bit. The white dress seemed too innocent. I'm not sure why, but it's suddenly important that Matteo doesn't view me as this innocent girl, but as a woman. A woman who knows what she wants, and isn't afraid to work for it.

Now I just need to figure out what it is I want when it comes to the tall, dark, and dreamy man I can't stop thinking about.

9

THE VESPA

Matteo

I MAY OR MAY not have bought a second helmet for my Vespa as soon as I left the bakery this morning.

Seeing her almost did me in. I didn't think I was going to be able to walk away. I could barely breathe. I don't know what it is about her that makes her so special. I haven't even spoken to her that much.

She has this way of getting under my skin, in my thoughts, and consuming my dreams.

I woke up rock hard this morning. I dreamt of her all night. I dreamt of what she would feel like under me. Of the sounds she would make. Of the way it would feel when we came together as one. I reach down to adjust myself in my pants. I've got to stop thinking that way or I'll wreck my Vespa.

As I make my way to Alda's bed and breakfast I can't help but wonder how on earth I got to this point. Desperate enough to spend basically every other night for three weeks with someone I know I shouldn't have anything to do with.

How did I get so desperate for my dad's approval? How did it come to the point my success is now dependent on his approval? It shouldn't matter. I should just go off and do it on my own. I have the funds and the ability. Then I can show him how much better things could be if he would just trust me.

I can't do that though. I don't want to do it without him. I couldn't possibly bring myself to do it without his approval and support. I just wish I could find a way to make him see my point of view.

If that means spending time with a woman who makes me want to forget everything I'm working for and ride off into the sunset, then so be it. I just have to stay strong. That's going to be easier said than done though. Especially since I almost couldn't control myself at the bakery this morning. How embarrassing.

I made sure to alleviate some tension in the shower before coming to pick her up. Maybe that will help keep me and my dick in line. One can hope anyway. No. I have to. I can't afford to get distracted. And I know once I get a taste I may never let her go. Then she'll have all the power to break me when she leaves. They always leave.

I pull up in front of the building and turn the engine off. I jump off and use my foot to pull out the kickstand. I take off my helmet and hang it on the handle bars.

I run my fingers through my hair as I walk through the front door. I find Alda standing behind the reception desk. She looks up from the papers on the desk and smiles. "It's been too long, young man. You need to come by for dinner again soon."

She makes her way around the front of the desk to greet me with a proper hug. We pull away and I return her smile as I take off my sunglasses. "Of course! It's been at least a few weeks since I've been here." I glance around the space that hasn't changed at all.

"Rosalie around?" I purposely don't make eye contact with her. She has always been so perceptive. I don't want her catching on to my feelings that I may or may not have for Rosalie, feelings I don't even understand myself.

She returns to her previous spot behind the desk and starts flipping through some papers. "She'll be right down. Juli is helping her with a few finishing touches." She looks up from her papers to give me a knowing smile. Shit.

If she looks any better than she did last night sitting in my restaurant, I may need to go home to change my pants before we go to dinner. I turn toward the stairs in the dining room when I hear Juli and Rosalie making their way to the reception area.

I'm pretty sure my heart stops beating when I see Rosalie in that white dress. She looks stunning.

We seem to find ourselves caught in a staring match. Neither of us want to look away and lose.

Juli gives a small giggle from beside Alda. I didn't even see her walk by me. I was too busy being caught up in Rosalie's magnetic pull.

"Doesn't she look beautiful tonight, Matteo?" That little snake. Juli knows exactly what she's doing. Poking the fire that has no business starting in the first place.

I avert my gaze with way too much difficulty to give Juli a look that most grown men would be afraid of. That just makes her smile grow. Perfect. I look toward the door and choose not to acknowledge Juli. "Where are we going tonight?"

"Lido." Rosalie walks out the door without any other comment. I still haven't managed to get my heart beating correctly after seeing her appear at the bottom of the steps.

I give Alda and Julie a little nod as I make my way out the door. "Ladies."

Before I can fully close it I can just make out Juli saying, "See! I told you they'll set the place on fire." I roll my eyes as I venture toward my Vespa that's parked by the curb.

Rosalie is standing by the door and makes a little gasp when she sees where I'm headed. I pull off the brand new helmet and try to hand it to her.

She takes a step back and shakes her head. "There's no way I'm getting on that thing with you. Don't you have a car we could take or something? I've seen how people ride those things through the traffic. Haven't you ever seen one of those fail videos where a Vespa driver gets hit by a car?" I open my mouth to answer, but I don't get the chance.

"No? Well I have. I'm not going to end up on a news site tomorrow morning. I can read the headlines." She starts pacing and moving her arms in a wild circle above her head. I decide to lean up against the Vespa to let her get it out of her system. Plus, it's kind of cute to watch if I'm being honest.

"American woman dies in a Vespa accident after agreeing to ride with a man she just met. Her heartbroken mother comes all the way to Italy to identify the body. Well, maybe heartbroken wouldn't be the right word. Maybe something generic? Grieving! That's it!" She starts to say something else but I cut her off as I push myself off the Vespa to stand.

"We didn't just meet. I've known you for forty-eight hours. Juli knows me, and you trust her judgment. I do own a car, but it's in the shop right now getting a new engine. I am a very careful driver. I've never even been in a car accident, let alone a Vespa accident." She's stopped moving now.

I give her a reassuring smile before I keep going. "We won't be going through the city, only back roads." I start to take a few steps in her direction while still talking. "And yes. I have watched those videos of Vespa accidents. But don't worry—" When I reach her, I take the bag off her shoulder. I assume it has her camera in it. I reach up and place the helmet on her head and buckle the strap. "You'll be safe with me." I finish it off with a little tug on the strap to tighten it up.

She's breathless now. "Okay," is all I get.

"Okay." I say as I start walking back to the Vespa to put my own helmet on. I put her bag in the storage compartment under the seat. "Come on, Rosa." I swing one leg over the seat to get on the scooter. I look over and extend my hand to help her get on the back. She looks at my hand, then back up to meet my eyes.

"Do you trust me?" I glance down at my hand to give her encouragement to take it. She pauses for a moment. She doesn't answer. She just takes my hand and swings her leg over the seat to tuck herself behind me.

She hesitates to put her arms around my middle. I reach around and take each hand and place them over my stomach. She lets out another little gasp that makes my dick stand at attention. "You have to hold on tight." I unlock the kickstand and start the engine. She rests her cheek on my back and my breath catches. What is this woman doing to me? I could get used to this, but I shouldn't. She'll only be here for three weeks. I just need to keep reminding myself of that.

I grind my teeth until I'm sure they're ready to crack. Don't get attached. I can't afford to get attached to someone who can't stay. I don't know if I can trust her even if she did. She would leave eventually. These three weeks need to go by quickly. I need to help her with the article, and we both need to move on. It'll be easier that way.

"You ready, Rosa?"

"Ready."

But what if I'm not?

10

DID YOU ENJOY THE RIDE?

Rosalie

"DO YOU TRUST ME?"

Yes. Why? Why do I trust this man?

I don't know. This makes no sense.

I don't understand, but I reach my hand out to take his anyway, because that truth is drowning out every other reservation trying to take control.

I hope he can't feel how fast my heart is beating. I'm pressed so closely to his back I'm sure he can feel it. Please don't be able to feel it. I haven't been on a Vespa since I was fourteen. I have no idea why I agreed to get on this thing. For some reason I decided I trusted him enough to take a ride.

I did learn one thing about myself tonight though, I do trust Matteo Moretti. Even though I've only known him for a few days, I trust him. I saw the look of pure determination in his eyes. I knew he wouldn't let anything happen to me. Apparently my heart didn't get the memo though. I'm afraid if it beats any faster it will jump out of my chest.

The wind is whipping around us as we fly down the little road on the outside of the city. We've been on the road for about twenty minutes so we should be there soon. I don't know if I'm excited or disappointed about the ride coming to an end to be honest. Even though I'm absolutely terrified of riding on a Vespa, I have actually somewhat enjoyed myself.

It's not the ride itself I'm afraid of, it's the memories of my last ride that scare me. Matteo has been true to his word though. He has actually been pretty careful. Plus, being on the back of his Vespa with him... that's the best part.

We arrive at the restaurant a few minutes later. I dread pulling the helmet off because I know my hair will be a mess underneath. Poor Juli put all that work into the beautiful braids for nothing. As we pull into a parking spot, Matteo cuts the engine.

I hesitantly release my death grip from around his middle. If I was hurting him he didn't mention anything. Although I'm sure it would take a lot to hurt the man. He has quite the six pack hiding under his shirt. I did my best to keep my hands from exploring, but I'm only human. And let me tell you, hot damn.

He moves to hold out his hand to help me off the scooter. I wiggle my way off in the most unladylike manner imaginable, and he has the audacity to stand so gracefully it makes me wonder if he has ever taken dance lessons. Show off. He reaches over to unbuckle my helmet. "Did you enjoy the ride?"

My eyes snap up to meet his as I work hard to fix my hair. "Excuse me?" Why did my mind go there? He asked a perfectly innocent question.

"Was the Vespa ride as scary as you thought it would be?" He has the audacity to laugh at me. Or with me. I can't be sure because I am indeed laughing at myself.

Right. Innocent question. "It wasn't that bad. It was actually quite enjoyable." A smile slips free when I see the sparkle in his eyes at my reply. He gets my bag from the storage compartment and hands it to me. Thankfully our fingers don't touch. I don't think I can handle his heat. We turn to walk into the restaurant, neither of us willing to admit something is blooming between us.

We walk in to find a small room with eight tables and a small walk up bar at the back of the room. The walls are covered in light tan and sage green patterned wallpaper. There's a small hostess stand to the right with a beautiful blonde standing behind it.

She smiles when she sees us. Her smile grows even brighter when she sees Matteo. I have the sudden urge to take his hand so I can stake my claim. I somehow manage to stop myself before I completely ruin our little pact. Business only. Right. I can do that. Hopefully.

"Do you have a reservation?" She says without breaking eye contact with Matteo.

He doesn't pay her any mind however when he answers her. "Yes, under Rosalie Auclair. Let Mario know Matteo Moretti is here if you don't mind."

She doesn't take kindly to being ignored. She gives a very childish little huff before she grabs some menus and starts walking into the main dining room area. "Right this way."

Matteo shocks me by placing his hand at the small of my back to guide me to our table. The hostess gives another little huff—I'm sure she was delightful as a child—and walks away. I flinch when our feet touch under the small two-seater table. The fabric of his pants rub against my bare calf. I try and fail not to squirm under his touch. Either Matteo doesn't notice or he chooses to spare me the humiliation.

We each pick up our menu and start to look over the selection. Matteo doesn't even look up when he reads off his recommendations from the menu. I'm actually glad he is here. Most of the menu is in Italian. I nod my head at him as I pull out my notebook and camera from my bag. A moment later a waiter and another man appear at our table. The other man is average in every way. Average height, build, age, and looks. He would make a great spy as he would blend right into a crowd.

"Matteo! It's been so long! I'm so glad you got to come out to see me. And you brought such a beautiful young lady with you." He looks over at me and reaches down to take my hand. He kisses it and continues to hold it with one hand while he motions to Matteo with the other. "I'm so happy you are here."

Matteo stands to give him a proper handshake. "Mario! So good to see you. The new menu looks great."

Mario gestures to me. "Aren't you going to introduce me to your lovely lady friend?"

I can feel the air thicken around Matteo. He obviously doesn't know what to say to that. Typical.

I take matters into my own hands. "I'm Rosalie. Matteo is so kindly giving me a food tour of the area for a magazine article I'm writing."

Mario gives us a big smile and brings his hands together in front of him like he's praying. "What magazine do you write for? This is just marvelous! Such great timing too! We just released our new menu!"

"I work for Foodie. I'm so excited to try one of your famous casseroles."

"Oh how wonderful! I hope you enjoy your dinner. I'll have some wine brought out for you both. On the house." Mario gives us a little bow and walks back toward the door that seems to lead into the kitchen.

Matteo sits back down and we both place our orders. After the waiter leaves I busy myself taking notes and photos while we wait for our salads. I want to make sure I really capture the essence of the place.

When I first arrived in Italy I thought I would only write about the food, but now I just don't think that would do the chef's justice. I need to show the entire picture. The atmosphere, the people, and the food. I look up to glance around the restaurant to see if I want to take a photo of anything else before the food comes. I catch Matteo staring at me. "What? Is there something on my face?" I start running my fingers over my face to find the culprit.

He sits forward in his seat and reaches out to push my hands off my face. "You don't have anything on your face. You're just very interesting to watch." I can feel the blush creeping up my chest and neck. Matteo notices too. He follows its path until he reaches my eyes once again. "Explain to me what you're doing, Rosa."

"Why do you call me Rosa instead of Rosalie?" I've wondered for a while. I just couldn't bring myself to ask, because I kind of like it.

He reaches forward to run two fingers gently across my cheek. I shiver when he makes contact. "When we first met your cheeks turned the color of a rose when you almost fell." My face must be the color of a tomato now. I don't get a chance to think about what he said too much, because the waiter arrives with our salads.

I catch the waiter before he leaves. "Could I get some extra dressing please?" He gives me a nod before walking away. We both unroll our napkins and place them in our laps. I take a few photos of my salad while I wait for the waiter to return.

My father used to say I like a little lettuce with my dressing. I can't help it. The dressing is the best part. The waiter brings my extra dressing and I dump it all on my salad only to realize it's still not enough. I half-raise my hand to motion for the waiter again, but decide to stick with the dressing I have at the last minute. I don't want to be a nuisance.

Matteo pushes his half empty dressing bowl over to me. I look up at him to try and figure out what he wants me to do with it. You can't possibly enjoy a salad with that little dressing.

"Take it." A little jerk of the head toward the dressing bowl is my only answer. Fine. I won't let good dressing go to waste. I pick up my fork to take my first bite, but I notice Matteo still hasn't eaten any of his. "Is there something wrong?"

He pushes his salad toward me. "Do you want to take a photo of mine as well?"

I set my fork down and pick up my camera. I can't believe he thought of that. "Thank you. Most people I eat with get upset when I ask to take photos of their food."

I quickly take the photo so he can begin eating. I slide the bowl back over to him. He surprises me again by taking a few scoops of his salad and placing it on a small plate that's supposed to be for the bread.

He slides that over to me as well. "You can't write about something you haven't tried." Now I'm really amazed. I shouldn't be, though. He is a chef after all. He must be used to trying new food with other chefs like this.

I try both of our salads and continue making notes. He startles me when he says, "Explain what you're doing, Rosa."

I put my favorite red pen down to replace it with my fork so I can fix the dressing throughout my salad. "I like to take notes about what I'm eating so I don't forget certain details. I also like to take photos of the dish to add to my article later. Most people like looking at photos of dishes rather than just reading a description." I take a bite of his salad next, then scribble down some notes.

Matteo doesn't say anything for a few moments. He seems deep in thought until he asks, "Would you like to see the kitchen before we leave?"

Would I ever! I could ask so many questions, and take some really cool photos for the article. "That would be great! Thank you. How do you know Mario anyway?" I take another sip of my wine.

"He used to work at Moretti's. He left to open his own restaurant a few years back." I give him a small nod as we finish off our salads.

The waiter shows up to replace our empty salad plates with our main course. Again, Matteo allows me to take a photo of his dish, and scoops out a few bites for me to try.

I take my first bite of the chicken tetrazzini casserole. I close my eyes and moan, enjoying the mixture of flavors. The mushroom, onion, and garlic are the stars of the show.

When I finally open my eyes I'm met with light in Matteo's eyes. "How did you become such a food connoisseur?"

I push my hair behind my shoulder, suddenly feeling warm. "It was just my dad and I when I was growing up. He tried so hard to cook for us at home, but he would always end up burning something and we would have to go out to eat instead. We became more and more adventurous as time went on, so I grew to like a variety of foods."

I smile to myself as I think back on those wonderful memories. "As you can imagine growing up in a small town, we didn't have much of a variety to choose from. We would always go on weekend trips together so we could try new places. We had a few favorites of course. This diner downtown was always a hit. We would always get them to make the strangest pancake toppings."

He lays his fork down. His food untouched. "What about your mom? Did she ever go with you?"

I shake my head. "No, but that was fine with me."

His laugh isn't one of humor. "I understand that all too well."

I tilt my head to the side, curious what caused his sudden shift. "You don't have a good relationship with your mom?"

He laughs again, still void of humor. "That's an understatement."

I nod my head, aware the topic has struck a nerve. "Tell me about how this casserole is made. I'd love to include that kind of stuff in my article."

I see the tension leave his shoulders almost immediately. He grabs my notebook and starts writing the ingredients. Talking me through them as he goes.

"I'll share my best kept secret. Most people only use butter when they first add the mushrooms, garlic and onions to the pan to cook. The trick is to season the butter while it's melting, then the dish is unforgettable."

Unforgettable. What a great word.

11

THAT ONE'S JUST FOR ME

Matteo

I CAN'T STOP LOOKING at her. She is a fascinating creature. I don't even think she realizes she mumbles to herself while she works. My new favorite thing may be this adorable little crease she gets between her brows when she's trying to figure out the best word to use in her notes.

I feel like a creeper. I don't seem to be making her uncomfortable though. I guess that's a good thing because I'm currently following her around like a lost puppy as we take a tour of the kitchen.

Mario opens the large walk-in freezer in the back of the room. Rosalie turns and gives me a face-splitting grin and does a little wiggle to further emphasize how excited she is. She is the cutest thing I've ever seen.

It's a little cramped in there, so I reach over and take her bag off her shoulder to hold while she goes in with Mario. I didn't even question the notion. It feels like the most natural thing in the world.

I don't know how, but this woman has turned my world upside down within a few days time. My willpower to ignore her pull is slowly fading. I don't know how much longer I will be able to hold out. I'm starting to question my sanity to be honest.

How can spending an hour watching one woman work make me change my mind about something so important to me? Not fully change my mind, just make me see things in a different way. What if I allowed myself to claim her? Just for three weeks. Maybe then I could get her out of my system. Or she could destroy me. Somehow I know she has the power to ruin me for anyone else.

I'm transported back to reality when the freezer door slams shut. I hand Rosalie back her bag, and we continue on our tour. After the tour she asks Mario countless questions, then we say our goodbyes and make our way toward the front door. I don't think she has stopped smiling since we entered the kitchen. I hold the door open for her to walk out.

She turns to look at me when we get to my Vespa. "Thank you so much for all of this. I never would have gotten to ask all those questions or tour the kitchen without you here."

I reach over to take her bag to store under the seat. "It's no problem. I'm glad I could help. I'll give you a tour of my kitchen soon." I grab her helmet and strap it on while she babbles about the food, Mario, and her interview with some of his staff.

I interrupt her while she takes a pause to suck in a deep breath. "The three C's." I start to count them off on my fingers. "Conversation, company, and cuisine. They're all equally as important to the dining experience." That seems to have stopped her brain from firing on all cylinders for the moment, so I take the brief pause to explain. "They're all equally as important. If one of the C's are bad, then the entire experience can be ruined. It's about the entire experience, not just the food."

It seems she has short circuited. I reach over to push a stray hair behind her ear, and then I hear her whisper. "You're amazing." What the hell. I drop my hand back to my side. I couldn't have heard her correctly. She suddenly shakes her head as if to physically clear the commotion going on inside her beautiful head. "Oh my gosh, did I say that out loud?" She's pacing now. She does that a lot.

I grab her hand to still her. I bring my other hand up to trace her lips with my thumb. She gives me a shaky inhale when I touch her bottom lip. "Yes, Rosa." I take a step toward her so we're sharing the same air. "You said that out loud."

Restraint I didn't know I was capable of is all that's keeping me from claiming her mouth. We're stuck in each other's gravity, and I can't bring myself to give a damn.

"I'm sorry. I shouldn't have said that. I'm sure Emilia wouldn't appreciate that."

"Why the hell would she care about what I do?"

"She's your girlfriend."

I shake my head. "I've never even met the girl."

"But I heard what you said at the train station."

It takes me a moment to recall what she could possibly be talking about. She couldn't have overheard what Luca and I were talking about. "Luca was trying to get me to go on a double date with him. Emilia is his girlfriend's best friend."

She moves closer to me. "So you're not dating anyone?"

I shake my head and lightly grab her waist. "No." My mouth is inches from hers. "I'm not dating anyone."

The spell is broken when the restaurant door bursts open and a family with a screaming baby walks out. We both spring apart like we're on fire. I have no idea what just happened. Rosa turns away from me and lets out a shaky breath.

The rolling hills in the distance must capture her attention. She grabs her camera and starts taking photos of the landscape. She gets this thoughtful look on her face before she goes over and picks a rose from a planter in front of the restaurant. I watch her try to position the rose in front of her camera so it's in the foreground of her shot. She's having a difficult time holding her camera and the rose though. Before I know it, my feet are moving on their own accord. I reach out and gently take the rose from her fingers. "Show me what to do."

"Thank you," she says quietly as she grabs my arm to position my hand the way she wants. She snaps a few photos before stepping back to look at the camera screen.

She starts to put her lens cap on to put her camera away, but I grab her hand to stop her. "Don't I get to see it?"

She doesn't say a word. She just hands me her camera so I can look at the screen. The photograph is good. Really good actually. It's not as stereotypical as I would have thought it would be. The mountains are actually out of focus. She focused on the smallest little split in a petal of the rose. I hadn't even noticed the flower was damaged. I hand her back the camera and look into her eyes because I want her to know how serious I am. "This is really good, Rosa. Will you put that photo in your article?"

She turns to look back at the mountains. "No. This one is just for me."

"Well that's a shame. Something that good deserves to be seen. You should start a blog or something so others can see your perspective."

I take a step toward her, but I turn just before I can reach her to grab my helmet from the handle bars, and swing my leg over the scooter. I've got to get the hell out of here before I kiss this woman. Rosalie quickly gets on the back, much more gracefully this time and without complaint.

Neither of us say a word as I push the kick stand back and start the engine. I get out on the main road and gun it toward the city. What the fuck happened back there?

Rosalie

What the hell happened to just business? I've been swept up in the tornado that is Matteo Moretti and I'm afraid I'll never be the same. This attraction is like nothing I've ever experienced before. It's unnatural to be honest. It doesn't make any sense.

Everything I thought I knew about Matteo was flipped on its head tonight. I thought he was grumpy, unkind, and thoughtless. He proved me so wrong.

Now I'm beginning to rethink this only business deal we have going on. What if we just had fun together while I'm here? No strings kind of thing. I know people do that all the time. Granted, I've never done anything like that.

Who am I kidding? There's no way that would work with Matteo. This attraction is too strong. It would break me. I can't let that happen. I won't.

I must have been deep in thought for a while, because we suddenly pull to a stop and Matteo cuts the engine in front of Alda's.

I unwrap my arms from around him and immediately miss his warmth. I reach up and unbuckle my helmet. He stands and takes my helmet to place on the handle bars. He digs my bag out of his storage compartment and hands it to me. Neither of us have spoken. We haven't even made eye contact.

Matteo breaks the silence when I turn away from him to start walking inside. "Hey listen." He reaches up to rub the back of his neck like he's nervous. He still won't make eye contact with me. "I'm sorry about all that back there. It was really unprofessional of me. It won't happen again." Right. I knew he hadn't changed his mind. Why would he?

"Let's just forget anything happened. Pick me up at the same time tomorrow?"

He lets out a sign of relief, but his face doesn't match. Do I see a hint of disappointment? No. I must be imagining things. "Yeah. Sure. I'll be here. Goodnight, Rosa."

"Goodnight." I make my way inside and close the door. He never moves from his spot. He doesn't even start the Vespa until I'm all the way upstairs and in my room. What a weird night.

I undress and take a quick shower. I still have an hour or so before I want to head to bed, so I grab my camera and transfer my photos over to my computer for safe keeping. While they are downloading I look through my photos from the past few days.

Maybe Matteo is right. I should share these photos with the world.

I spend some time researching blog sites before I finally pick one. Before I know it, I've spent two hours customizing my own blog. My first entry reads kind of like a diary. It's not like anyone will read this anyway.

I finish the post off with the photo I took of the front of Alda's place and a few photos of her gallery wall downstairs. Azzurro and its people are slowly stealing my heart.

I put the finishing touches on my first post before I head to bed for the night.

Isle of Capri

There's a few things that have surprised me about Italy so far. How everything seems to be brighter, how the people seem to be happier, and how much I love it here.

My host may be one of my favorite new friends. She told me this morning over breakfast about the story behind this place. She wanted to open the inn because she grew up helping her grandfather with his inn on the Isle of Capri.

She came to Azzurro alone for university when she was only seventeen. She even took all the photographs that can be found throughout the rooms. She started this bed and breakfast all on her own. I hope I can be like her some day.

12

WHEN IN ROME

Matteo

LUCA LEANS BACK IN the chair in my office and gives me a smirk before digging in. "So what are you going to do about it?"

Here we go. I roll my eyes as I look up from the mountain of papers on my desk and act like I have no idea what he's talking about. "Do about what?"

He sits forward in his seat to look me dead in the eye. "Rosalie, of course. She has to be what's gotten you in such a bad mood. You've been snapping at everyone since I got here today, you almost made Enzo cry earlier, and your dad says you've been acting weird for the past week. That timing lines up pretty well with a certain brunette with nice legs coming to town. Just go for it man. What's that saying? When in Rome."

My head snaps up and I point a finger at him. "Don't talk about her legs unless you have a death wish. And leave me the fuck alone."

He jumps up out of his seat like he's been shot and wags a finger in my face. "See! That right there! That's what I'm talking about. I mean, you're always grumpy, but you've taken it to an entirely different level."

I lean back in my seat. I've gotten so behind on work it's not even funny. I've been snapping at all my employees for absolutely no reason. Hell, I don't even want to be around me. I don't want to hear about it from Luca though, so my best option is to deflect the conversation back at him. "When do you go back to Naples again? Shouldn't you be visiting your mom or something?"

He laughs. That dick. "Ah come on. You obviously need me. You're a mess. I've never seen a woman get to you like this man. So, what are you going to do about it?"

I have no idea. It's been a week. Seven damn days of torture. I pick her up, we go to dinner, we carry on with small talk, and I drop her back at Alda's. I've really enjoyed my time with her to be honest. I can barely work each day because I'm thinking about seeing her at night for dinner. I've learned all about her mom, and her obsession with trying new ice cream flavors. I've also learned a lot about her life in New York, which is the exact reason why we could never work.

Our relationship would have an expiration date. A short one at that. We have twelve days. That's hardly enough time to get tired of a song, let alone figure out if you want to have a relationship with someone. Not just a relationship, but a long distance relationship.

Luca breaks my train of thought when he sighs loudly and sits back in his seat with a huff. "Alright. Spill." He gestures with his hand for me to get going. Fine.

"I don't know man. She's killing me. My favorite part of my day is when I go pick her up. She ate dinner at Alda's Thursday instead of our usual thing and I thought I was going to ruin the rug in my living room from pacing. I almost invited myself just so I could see her, but I didn't want to sound desperate. At this point I'll do just about anything to make her laugh. I'm even giving her my salad dressing. What the hell has happened to me?"

Luca gets a confused look on his face. "You give her your salad dressing?" I'm the one to stand up now. I've got to do something with all my nerves, so I start pacing the tiny space.

"Don't ask. Please spare me. I'm pretty sure she put a spell on me or something." I stop pacing when Luca starts laughing so hard he has tears running down his face. I cross my arms and glare at him. "What the hell is your problem?"

That just makes the laughing worse. He's wiping the tears from his eyes when he says, "Ah shit. You've got it bad man. Real bad."

Now I'm confused. "What the hell are you talking about?" I sit back down because I'm suddenly feeling light headed.

He's still laughing. "You're catching feelings man."

No. Definitely not. I hardly know her. I will admit though, there is something between us. I just don't know if I can trust her enough to put the effort into figuring out what it is. She'll leave in twelve days. Twelve fucking days.

What the hell am I going to do?

Rosalie

"Girl, you are so screwed." Oh don't I know it. I'm sitting across from Juli while we eat lunch at Alda's. My only response is laying my head on the table and groaning. I can't seem to find the energy to do anything more. All my energy is being consumed by writing my new blog, writing my article for Foodie, and Matteo Moretti.

Juli throws a grape at me. "Get up. Oh poor Rosalie. I don't know how to deal with my feelings for a hunk of a man who owns his own business and makes me feel weak in the knees. What ever will I do?" She's making an exaggerated sad face. "Enough with the pity party. Just tell him how you feel." She shrugs like that's the easiest thing in the world.

I sit up and dust the imaginary crumbs off the table cloth. "You know I can't do that. I'll only be here for another twelve days. I'll be leaving and I'll probably never see him again. That's not fair to either of us."

Admitting defeat she sits back in her chair and sighs. "Fine. I know things are complicated, but maybe long distance would work?"

I get up and start pacing the length of the dining room. "You don't think I haven't thought of that?" I start moving my arms around above my head. "Relationships are hard enough without adding long distance to the mix."

Alda walks by with a basket of fresh folded towels. She sets them down on the table and puts her hands on her hips. "Have you even kissed the man?" What the hell? I stop pacing to stare at her for a moment before I look over at Juli. All she gives me is a shrug. That's not at all what I thought she was going to say. *Have you seen the live action of Beauty and the Beast? Have you ever tried clams? Maybe even, have you ever colored your hair?* But definitely not that.

"Well no," is all I can say as I sit back down at the table. I put my elbows on the table so I can use them to hold my head up. I need all the help I can get.

"Well you're getting all worked up for nothing. Kiss the man and see if you like it. If you don't, then there's nothing to worry about. If you do, then we will figure out what to do." She gives me a little nod and picks up her basket to start walking up the stairs. I'd offer to help her, but she would only shoo me away. Stubborn woman.

Juli stands so she can reach the grapes at the other end of the table. "She has a point, you know. Maybe you should just kiss him and see how it goes." She gives me a little pat on the hand before she refills her plate of grapes.

"What am I supposed to do, sneak attack him at the dinner table? Run outside when he gets here and jump on him? Yell 'Take me Matteo, I'm yours?'"

She almost chokes on the grape she just popped in her mouth. "Now I would pay good money to see that. That's not what I had in mind though. Just kiss him if the moment is right."

I roll my eyes at my new friend. "Could you be any more vague?" I reach for a grape on her plate and pop it in my mouth.

"Just go with it. No stress."

I shake my head at her and laugh. Maybe she has a point though. Whatever is going on between Matteo and I may only be surface level. I guess there's one way to find out. Hopefully a kiss won't ruin everything though. I look at Juli with wide eyes. "But what if he breaks off our pact because I kiss him?"

She gives me a little grimace. "I didn't think about that. Maybe it's not such a good idea then."

We finish off our plate of grapes, and she grabs my arm as she stands. "Come on. Let's go take a walk. I think you need some fresh air."

I get up and smooth out the wrinkles on my sage green sundress. "Maybe we can get some photos for my new blog?"

I do know one thing for certain, I will have a difficult time getting on that plane in twelve days. No matter what happens with Matteo, it breaks my heart to think about leaving these amazing people.

13

SOAKING WET

Rosalie

MATTEO AND I ARE going to one of Juli's top picks for dinner tonight.

We're getting a later start than normal because Matteo had to finish something up at work. So I had plenty of time to kill waiting for him to arrive. Unfortunately, that means we won't have much time at the restaurant.

I'm sitting in my room working on my next blog post when I hear his Vespa pull up out front. I save my progress, and take one last look in the mirror. I'm still in my sage green sundress from earlier, but I dressed it up with some strappy heels and a nice necklace. I smooth my loose curls out before I make my way downstairs.

Alda is standing outside talking to Matteo when I reach the front door.

She gives me a hug before I make my way toward the Vespa. "I was just telling Matteo it's going to rain tonight."

He shakes his head and smiles at her. "And I was just telling her the forecast is clear."

She shakes her head right back. "My knees have always been a better judge of the coming weather." She points at me. "Mark my words. You will be soaking wet when you come home tonight." She gives me a little wink and walks back inside.

Did she really just say soaking wet with a wink? I try my best to not make eye contact with Matteo. He just laughs and hands me my helmet.

Alda's comment about the weather makes me realize something. "How long does it take to replace an engine anyway? Surely it should have been done by now."

"It should be done soon."

Well that wasn't much of an answer. Oh well. I don't even own a car, so what do I know?

I strap the helmet on and situate myself behind him. I thought the shock of being pressed against him like this would wear off, but I couldn't have been more wrong. It's like my entire body is humming when we touch. I reach my arms around his middle and lay my cheek on his back. We both let a small sigh slip free when I'm settled.

I breathe in the now familiar sandalwood and leather as he starts the engine. "Do you think we should be worried about the weather?"

He shakes his head and pulls out onto the road. He has to talk louder over the sound of the engine. "No. I think we'll be fine. The skies are clear and I didn't see anything on the weather forecast this morning." He pats my hands that are resting against his stomach. "Don't worry, Rosa."

After making it to the restaurant we take our seats at a reserved table, because of course, Matteo knows the head chef. I suspect he is why we got a reservation in the first place.

The tension is thick as the hostess leaves us. Neither of us have said a word since we left Alda's.

I unfold my napkin and place it in my lap just so I can have something to do with my hands. I look everywhere but at him. I'm pretty sure if we make eye contact I will self-combust and that would be a horrible end to my lovely trip.

I decide to break the ice while I try the bread. "So, how is Luca?" I hope my tone of voice comes across more normal than it sounds in my head, like I'm desperate for a reprieve from the heat unfurling between us.

I make the mistake of looking over at him when he takes a slow sip of his water. I can't help but track the movement in his neck as he swallows, and the tightening of the muscles in his arm as he places the glass back on the table. He has the sleeves of his button-up rolled up to his elbows and his black watch stands out against his white shirt and light gray slacks. I can't take my eyes off of him.

I keep watching as he runs a hand through his hair and licks his lips. He finally answers my question. "Luca is good; he's excited to be home for a few days. His mom is throwing him a birthday party next weekend and he asked me to invite you, Juli, and Alda. He's not thrilled to be making the trip again so soon, but his mom insisted."

I nod my head as I take a sip of my water. "I would love to come. I was hoping I would get to see him again before I go home. I'll let Juli and Alda know we've been invited."

The waiter arrives to take our order. I take Matteo's recommendation as always. After the waiter leaves, I excuse myself and go to the ladies' room. I need to compose myself before I pass out at the table. I haven't even taken any photos of the restaurant tonight. I have to remember why I'm here.

I splash some cold water on my cheeks and pat them dry. I look at myself in the mirror. What am I doing? I need to focus. I can't keep getting so worked up over a guy like this. It will ruin my chances of getting hired at Foodie.

I run my hands through my hair to smooth out the tangles from the ride here. After I'm done, I give myself a nod in the mirror. "You can do this." Geez. Now I'm talking to myself.

I decide confidence is key in this situation. I need to stay focused, and not let some outrageously gorgeous man distract me from my goals. So, I strut back to the table and sit down as gracefully as I possibly can. I grab my notebook and camera from my bag, and begin my usual process. When I look up at Matteo after a few minutes of working he steals my breath once again. The fire in his eyes is unmistakable. I have to squeeze my legs together to get some relief from the ache he always manages to cause.

I tuck a stray hair behind my ear and lick my lips. He follows the movement. I watch as the fire in his eyes turns into an inferno that is sure to destroy me.

The waiter suddenly appears and places our salads in front of us. The sudden intrusion causes us both to jump and break eye contact. The waiter gives me an apologetic smile. I guess he knows he just interrupted something. I'm surprised the entire restaurant hasn't been consumed by fire and left in a pile of ashes around us.

After a few moments Matteo breaks the silence. "How is your article going?" We still haven't made eye contact. That's probably for the best. I don't know if I will survive it.

"Not as well as I would have hoped at this point." My blog has taken up far too much of my time if I'm being honest. "I just can't seem to find my voice. Whenever I reread my progress so far it sounds like someone else wrote it."

I feel horrible about it. Matteo has taken so much time away from his restaurant to help me with transportation. I know my experience wouldn't have been anywhere near as beneficial without him. I'm not just talking about transportation though. I've gotten to tour kitchens, meet amazing chefs, and ask so many questions because of him.

I expect to see anger on his face when I finally take a chance and make eye contact with him. But instead, I'm greeted with confidence and understanding. "You'll find your voice, Rosa."

I feel like a weight has been lifted from me with those simple words. I smile and look down at my hands in my lap. "Thank you." He didn't give me any advice, or tell me what to do about the situation. He just believes in me. That's a great feeling I don't know if I'll ever be able to go without again.

He just gives me a small nod before he motions to my camera on the table. "Go on. Take your photos so we can eat." His smile reaches his eyes.

I grab my camera and get to work. While I take photos, I lighten the conversation up a bit. "So, how did you and Luca meet?"

He laughs and shakes his head. "Let me tell you a story about two little boys, a swing set, and some apple slices."

I listen intently. Seeing the light in his eyes as he talks fills a void in my chest I wasn't aware was there. I feel like I'm seeing the facade he has carefully constructed for everyone around him melt away. The true Matteo is being revealed.

I lean forward and raise my eyebrows. "Why didn't you just split your sandwich with him? That would have made way more sense."

He shakes his head, a grin firmly on his face. "I never said I was a nice person, Rosa."

"Yet here you are, offering to drive me all over for dinners and allowing me to take up all your time."

I take a sip of my drink, trying like hell to not show how much he affects me. My heart is racing as he stares back at me. Someone could drown in the depth of his sapphire gaze if they aren't careful.

"You forget, I'm getting something out of this too."

I sigh and move my gaze down to my lap. I should have known this was all only about ensuring his restaurant is mentioned in the article. "I know. The article."

He reaches out and grabs my hand with a feather light touch. A small gasp escapes me as I look up, startled by the contact. "No, Rosa. I get to spend time with you."

I feel a crease form between my brow as I open my mouth to speak. I am, however, interrupted by the waiter with our entree. He sets the food down in front of us. He gives us an aggravated look as he walks away, not even trying to hide his disdain. I glance at my phone to see we still have twenty minutes before closing.

Matteo pulls my attention back to the table as he pushes a plate to me with a small portion of his meal to try. "Don't forget to take your photos."

Right. Photos. I almost forgot. How silly of me.

I snap a few quick photos before I begin eating my meal. I doubt the photos will be usable since I can't seem to find the enthusiasm that normally comes with photography. For the first time in my life something else feels more important.

I put my camera away and look back up to find him watching me. "What's your favorite color, Rosa?"

I smile, "What? Is this twenty questions now?"

He leans forward and puts his elbows on the table, his chin resting on his folded hands. "If that's what it takes."

I tuck a stubborn strand of hair behind my ear. "Blue. What's your favorite season?"

"Summer. What's your favorite food?"

I answer quickly, "Bacon. What is your biggest pet peeve?"

"When parents let their kids run wild at a train station. If you could be an animal, what would you be?"

I lean forward slightly, my meal forgotten. "A lioness. If you had one day left to live, how would you spend it?"

"Sailing. If you could be a fictional character, who would you be?"

I can't keep the smile from my face. "Elizabeth Bennet. If you could pick a superpower, what would you choose?"

"Water breathing. What is the craziest thing you've ever done?"

"Skinny dipping. What's your biggest fear?"

He leans forward even more and shakes his head. "Oh no. You're not getting away with that one. I need details."

I shake my head and laugh as I lean back in my chair. "Nope."

His smile is practically taking over his face. "Ah, come on! You can't tell me you skinny dipped, and not follow through with the story."

It's at that exact moment the waiter decides to return with our check. He rolls his eyes and walks away. I sink down in my chair and do my best to cover my bright red face with my hand.

Matteo laughs as he stands. He holds his hand out to me, "Come on. We better get going."

I stand and gather my things while Matteo pays the bill. Matteo has his hand on the small of my back as he guides me through the front door toward his Vespa.

He leans down and whispers in my ear, "I'll get that story out of you eventually, Rosa. No use in hiding it."

I look up at him and smile innocently, "You'll have to catch me first."

I take off running in the direction of the Vespa with every intention of being caught. He catches me quickly, pulling my back to his chest and lifting me so he can spin me around.

We're laughing so hard I almost missed the thunder in the distance and the rain that is starting to fall lightly around us. We both stop and turn in the direction of the very mean looking storm that's off in the distance.

"Shit," Matteo says, just as we hear another crack of thunder a little louder than the one before. We both turn to see the restaurant staff lock the doors and head to their cars. We are at least forty-five minutes outside of the city. We only passed residential buildings on the way here. This is more of a venue rather than a traditional restaurant, so there's not much around for miles.

Matteo grabs my hand and starts quickly walking to the Vespa. "We've got to hurry if we don't want to get caught in the middle of that storm." We rush to stow my camera away under the seat—at least that compartment is waterproof. We quickly put on our helmets and before I know it we are speeding down the road with loud booms of thunder directly overhead.

I tighten my hold around Matteo's stomach and bury my head as much as I can behind his back.

I jump as a bolt of lightning streaks the sky and lands so close the hairs on the back of my neck stand up. There is no delay in the thunder. The storm is here, and I have no idea what we're going to do.

14

CLAIM ME

Matteo

WHAT THE HELL ARE we going to do? We can't stay on the road like this. We're sure to run into some flash flooding or crash because of horrible visibility. I can't believe I put Rosa in danger like this. I knew better. I should have listened to Alda, and not taken the chance with us being so far away from the city.

The hairs on the back of my neck stand as a large streak of lightning goes directly overhead. Rosalie jumps and I swear I'm about to lose my mind. Thankfully, the lightning gave me enough visibility to see a structure just up ahead. Hopefully someone is home and they'll let us in so we can wait out this storm. I spot a dirt road leading there, but it doesn't look promising. We don't have a choice though. We've got to get off the road.

As I pull around a large tree I quickly realize this place is abandoned. Oh well. This is really our only option at this point. I stop as close to the structure as I can get without getting the Vespa in the weeds. Rosalie jumps off and runs for the building taking her helmet off as she goes. I quickly follow her after I secure the kickstand and place my helmet on the handle bars. It's already soaked, so it doesn't matter that it'll be left in the rain.

I can see Rosalie struggling with something up ahead. Did she drop something? She's going to have to wait until this storm passes to find it if that's the case. The visibility out here is shit. When I reach her I realize one of her heels has sunken down in the mud and she can't free herself. Her helmet is on the ground. She must have dropped it when her heel got stuck.

She doesn't hear me coming from the pounding of the rain so I startle her when I reach down and yank her heel off. I pick her up bridal style and start walking toward the abandoned structure. "We'll get it later. We've got to get inside." She wraps her arms around my neck and buries her face under my chin. I feel so much better with her in my arms. Right where she belongs.

There's not a front door, just a hole where one once stood, so it's easy enough to make our way inside. There's debris laying all over the floor. I manage to find what looks to be a handmade bench and some camping chairs in the corner of the room. The bench is almost as big as a twin bed, and looks rather clean. I guess someone has been here more recently than I thought. There's also a few empty beer bottles. Hopefully this is just a hangout spot for some of the local kids.

I sit down on the bench and situate Rosa in my lap. Her legs are hanging on one side and her head is resting on my shoulder. She's shaking, which makes me want to punch something. I should never have put her in this situation. My selfishness could get her hurt. I lied to her earlier. My car has been at home for a few days now. I just didn't want to give up the opportunity to have her close. How could I be so thoughtless?

I pull her close to me to try and get her warm. Our clothes are soaked through. I mindlessly rub small circles on her back. "It'll be okay, Rosa. I won't let anything happen to us. We are safe here." I don't know if I'm trying to comfort her or myself. She shifts in my arms and inhales like she's about to say something. "What can I do to make it better?" I need her to tell me before I lose my mind.

She hesitates once again before she says so quietly I almost can't hear her, "I'm afraid of storms."

I tighten my grip around her. The need to keep this woman safe is overwhelming. "It's okay. We're all afraid of something. It's nothing to be ashamed of."

I can feel her shake her head against my chest. "You don't understand."

"Then help me understand."

She sighs and buries her head even deeper against my chest. "My dad died when I was fourteen." I tense at her words but I don't stop rubbing small circles on her back. She takes a moment before continuing. "We were visiting my grandparents in southern France for the summer. We rode on a Vespa to the coast for the day." Her hesitation to ride my Vespa suddenly makes sense.

"We took a sailboat out. Just my dad and I. We didn't go far off the coast. We just wanted to get a good view and swim for a while." She sniffs and wipes at her face with the back of her hand. I pull her even closer to me. I don't say a word as I wait for her to continue.

"A freak storm rolled in. It was pretty bad. Lots of lightning and heavy wind."

She lets out a shaky breath while she breaks my heart.

"We lost control of the boat. We almost capsized and I fell overboard. My father rushed to help me back on the boat. I swam as hard as I could toward him. He fell overboard as he was pulling me over the railing. I had a life jacket on, but he didn't. I've been afraid of storms ever since."

I feel like my heart is in my throat. "It took the rescuers eighteen hours to find me." That one sentence destroys me.

I shift her so I can look at her face. I need to look at her. Touch her. Neither of us speak as we take each other in for a few moments. She's so close but I can barely see her eyes because of the darkness surrounding us. "Thank you." She says so quietly I almost can't hear her over the rain beating on the roof.

"For what?" I'm still rubbing circles on her back because I can't stop touching her.

She catches a drop of water from my hair with her thumb as it runs down my cheek. "For rescuing me." This woman is going to ruin me. That doesn't bother me. Not one bit. Not anymore.

"Always." I almost lose my mind when I see the change in her eyes.

"Matteo?"

"Yes, Rosa?"

She moves so she's straddling me. I grab her head with both hands and stroke her bottom lip with my thumb. She lets out a little sigh that is almost my undoing. "Tell me to stop, Rosa."

"Claim me, Matteo, and don't you dare stop."

That's all the permission I need before I claim her mouth. One taste and I know I'm ruined forever.

I'm not gentle as I slide one arm around her waist and slide my other hand around to take control of her neck. In one swift movement I move her so she's laying on her back. She parts her mouth as an invitation I will gladly accept as I settle myself between her legs. Right where I belong. She doesn't hold back as she meets me kiss for kiss. She reaches her hands up to run her fingers through my hair and I groan into her mouth.

I slide both hands down until I find her plump ass and push her dress up her thighs. I slide my hands under her dress and up her tight body until I find the bottom edge of her bra. I gently squeeze her there as a silent plea for permission to keep going.

She nods her head and I sigh with relief. We don't break our kiss as I tease a nipple through the lace of her bra. I'm rewarded with a moan. That is my new favorite sound.

I continue to tease her nipple as I move my other hand down to take a palm full of her ass. I'm hard as steel as I rock against her. I've dreamt about this moment and my dreams could never compare to the reality of Rosa beneath me.

One touch and I know no other woman could ever compare. I stop before we go too far. "I'm taking you on a date." It's not a question.

My eyes have slightly adjusted to the darkness, so I can clearly see her expression now. I search her face for any sign that what just happened was as powerful for her as it was for me. I'm met with certainty and longing. She gives me a little nod before she answers. "Absolutely."

15

WHERE DID YOU COME FROM?

Rosalie

WE HAVEN'T MOVED. I'M laying on the bench, and Matteo is hovering over me. I agreed to go on a date with him and I don't regret it. Not yet anyway. We only have twelve days, but I know I'll regret it for the rest of my life if I don't take what little time we've been given.

I know my heart will be broken in the end, but it'll be worth it. I hope so anyway.

Matteo sits up and pulls me with him so I'm sitting in his lap. He strokes my bottom lip with his thumb. "Do you hear that?"

"No." I can't concentrate on anything but him though, so I'm probably not the best person to ask. A dinosaur could probably walk in and I would be none the wiser.

"Exactly. The rain has stopped." He stands with ease.

I instinctually wrap my legs around his middle so I don't fall. He places a hand on my bottom to stabilize me. "I can walk, you know." I say with a giggle, even though I'm perfectly happy right where I am.

"With one heel? There's probably broken glass all over this place. He looks down with a challenge in his eyes and raises one eyebrow.

I give a fake huff of defeat. It's not very convincing, because I haven't stopped smiling since our kiss. Who am I kidding, that was more than a kiss. We basically had sex with our clothes on.

He rewards me with a deep laugh as he carries me out of our little sanctuary and back into the real world. I can still hear the rumble of thunder in the distance, but the sky is clear above us. The moonlight shines so brightly compared to the darkness inside the shack we were just in, and I feel like I've walked out into midday sun.

He sets me down on the Vespa before he goes back over to my buried shoe and my muddy helmet. He squats down to inspect the damage. He pinches the only visible strap with two fingers and pulls it from the mud.

"I'm afraid it's ruined." He stands to walk over and show me.

He's right. There's no saving it. Oh well. I found them at a thrift store in SoHo. I take the heel from him and toss it into the mountain of trash next to the shack. I know it's technically littering, but no one is going to notice the addition of just one heel. Plus, it's not like I can hold it on the way back to the city.

Matteo laughs and bends down to give me a quick kiss on the forehead. I feel the kiss throughout my entire body. "Let's get going before we get caught in another storm and you try to strip me of my clothes."

I give him a play slap on the arm as he fastens his helmet. He wipes my helmet off on his shirt. "Don't act like you didn't enjoy our detour. I could tell you enjoyed yourself." I gesture to his very impressive package still straining against his slacks. I finish it off with a wiggle of my eyebrows for good measure. Now he's really laughing.

"Oh I liked it, Rosa. I can guarantee you that." He takes a step in my direction to secure my wet helmet. "That's why we're going on a date tomorrow. I can't wait much longer."

His statement makes my toes tingle. I don't know if I can wait any longer either. It feels like we are at a race against the clock. Like the hour glass has been turned upside down and our time together is being taken away by the filling sand.

"Pick me up in the morning. It's Sunday, you have the day off."

"Do you have my schedule memorized, Rosa?"

He gives me a playful grin before he situates himself on the scooter in front of me. I wrap my arms around his middle and lay my cheek on his very damp shirt. He grabs my hands and gives me a squeeze before he starts the engine.

On the way back into the city I work my hands under his shirt so I can feel him. When my hands make contact with his bare chest I feel his muscles tighten and spasm. I love that I'm the one getting this reaction out of him. Something tells me Matteo is not easily flustered.

I keep my hands there until we pull up in front of Alda's. He cuts the engine just as Alda and Juli come running out the front door. Well Juli runs, Alda just meanders down the steps like she doesn't have a care in the world.

Juli reaches me first and gives me a hug even though I'm soaked to the bone. I reluctantly let go of Matteo to return her hug.

"You scared us to death! I tried calling. I'm so glad you're alright."

It feels good to have someone worry about me for once. "I'm sorry. My phone was in my bag under the seat. I didn't even think about texting when we got back to the Vespa."

We separate from the hug just as Alda joins us. She looks between me and Matteo with a knowing smile on her face. "I knew you'd be coming home soaking wet. Let's get you inside and dry you off."

She gives me a wink before coming over to pat my hand. I'm sure my face has turned a bright shade of red.

Matteo still hasn't said a word. He slides off the Vespa with the grace of a cheetah, and bends down to take off my remaining shoe. "You won't be needing this anymore."

He hands the solo heel to Juli, and she looks at it like it's a bomb about to go off. Alda and Juli stand silently and watch as Matteo scoops me into his arms and carries me through the front door. Juli looks over to Alda with a look of confusion on her face. Alda just gives her a smile and pats her on the shoulder. Alda starts following us, but I guess it takes a moment for Juli's feet to cooperate.

"What is your room number?" Matteo asks me.

"Four. All the way at the end."

When we reach my room I help him open the door. He doesn't put me down until we are standing in my bathroom. He sets me down on the small vanity. We still haven't spoken. His face has turned even more serious than usual. I watch his muscles tense under his shirt. He's facing away from me when he finally speaks. "My mother abandoned my father and I when I was fifteen."

I'm shocked, but I don't say anything. He doesn't need my pity. He just needs someone to listen. He swallows slowly before he continues.

"She went to visit her sister in Chicago one winter while we were living in Florida. She fell on some ice, and her knee and wrist got pretty messed up. She had three surgeries, and was put on pain pills." He turns so he's fully facing me. The look of anguish on his face takes my breath away. He slowly turns away from me to face the door. "After a year of rehab she was completely healed. She no longer needed the pain pills, but she didn't stop taking them. Soon, pain pills weren't enough, so she turned to alcohol. That led to other drugs, and before my father and I knew it, she wasn't my mom anymore."

I listen, wanting so badly to reach out and comfort him.

"My father never gave up on her though. Even though she sold the house, the car, and basically everything she could get her hands on so she could support her drug habit. The title to the house and car were in her name. She even started shoplifting so she could sell that stuff too."

My heart breaks for this man. This wonderful man.

"She overdosed one night while my dad was at work. We were living in a cheap hotel, and my dad was working three jobs to try and pay for my mom's treatment. She had gone to rehab so many times it was difficult to find any financial help. I called the police after she passed out. She almost died, and that still wasn't a wakeup call. My dad checked her into a rehab facility that night. She left three days later. I haven't seen her since."

He moves so he's standing with his palms on the door and his head is hung low. "After she left, my dad packed up what little we had left and we came back to Italy."

I walk over and wrap my arms around him from behind. "Your dad sounds like a wonderful man."

He lets out a shaky breath before he turns to look at me. He puts both hands on either side of my face and searches my eyes. "Where did you come from?" He asks softly.

My answer is standing on my tiptoes and kissing him. I kiss him so hard I see stars. He answers me tenfold. He spins me so my back is against the door. He's caging me in, but I've never felt more free. We kiss for what feels like an eternity of bliss before he breaks away to look me in the eye.

"I'll pick you up at nine in the morning. Wear comfortable shoes." He kisses my forehead, before pulling me away from the door and opening it. "Goodnight, Rosa." When he opens the hallway door, Alda and Juli are leaning against the opposite wall waiting.

They don't say a word. They just watch him walk down the hallway and disappear down the steps. No one moves until we hear the door close downstairs. Alda speaks up first. "I'll go make you some tea." She turns to walk down the hallway to the kitchen downstairs.

Juli rushes into my room and closes the door behind her. "Tell me everything."

Little does she know, I won't be telling her much of anything. What Matteo said was just for me.

16

NOTED.

Matteo

IT TAKES EVERY OUNCE of strength I have to walk down the stairs and out the front door. I want to walk back up the stairs and claim the rest of her just like she offered.

I won't do that though. Not tonight anyway. I want to do this right. She's not the type of girl you fuck and run. I don't think I could run away now even if I tried. I want to do right by her. She deserves that, because after our twelve days are up—I'm not going to think about that now. I want to focus on the time we have together. We can figure out everything else later.

As I drive away from the woman who has turned my life upside down, I know one thing for certain: she ruined me with one kiss. I'll never be the same.

9 a.m. can't come soon enough.

I arrive at Alda's the next morning with a strange feeling in my chest. I tossed and turned all night. Did I make the right decision opening up to her? Did I ruin everything by kissing her? I have worked myself up so much I didn't even eat breakfast this morning. I feel like a sixteen year old picking up his date for prom.

I run a hand through my hair and walk through the front door. Alda, Juli, and Rosalie are all sitting around the dining room table sipping coffee. The conversation stops when I enter, and Rosa turns to look at me. Alda says something, but I can't hear her over the roaring in my ears.

Rosa is a vision in high waisted jean shorts, a tank top that hits just below her belly button, and white sneakers. Her dark hair is curled and loose, floating down her back.

Alda comes up and pats me on the arm, breaking me from the spell Rosa put me under. "Would you like some breakfast?" She laughs under her breath as she gestures to the table piled high with food. I must have forgotten how to speak, because all I can do is shake my head no.

Rosa stands and gathers her small crossbody bag. It's not the normal one she brings with her for our dinners. I find my voice again enough to ask, "No camera today?"

She shakes her head as she walks in my direction. "Nope." She waves her phone at me. "Just my phone. I don't want to have to deal with a big camera today. My phone does just as good." She grimaces. "Well, for the most part anyway."

She walks up to me. She doesn't have heels on today, so she only comes up to my chin. I reach up and tuck a stray hair behind her ear. "Ready to go?"

Why are my hands tingling? And why is my heart beating so fast?

She nods her head and looks over her shoulder, and waves goodbye to Juli and Alda. "See you later."

They both wave and Juli says, "Have fun!" She adds a little squeal at the end. I roll my eyes at her as I wave goodbye. She shoots me the middle finger as I walk away.

We walk out the front door, and Rosa stops in her tracks. "Where's the Vespa? Are we walking? Is that why you wanted me to wear comfortable shoes?"

I laugh as I grab her by the shoulders to turn her toward my blue BMW M4. The color almost matches my Vespa. "Nope." I scratch the back of my neck. "I actually have a confession to make. The engine replacement has been done for a few days."

She turns to face me. "Why did you say it was still at the shop then?"

I can't make eye contact with her, so I decide to give my shoes a thorough inspection. "I liked having you wrapped around me." I have to force myself to make eye contact when I apologize. "I'm sorry, Rosa. I could have gotten us hurt last night."

She gives me a smile as she makes a circle around the car. "It would have been a shame to have this out in the rain last night." This woman. She stops in front of the passenger door. I return her smile as I walk around to open the door for her.

I've got to get some of my nerves out, so I take a chance. "Listen, about last night." I look down at her beautiful face. "I'm sorry if I came on too strong, and you felt uncomfortable in any—"

"You didn't make me feel uncomfortable." She gives me a smile that eases my mind.

She slides in and I hurry over to get in the driver's seat. When I get in, Rosa is inspecting the interior. "This is a pretty nice ride."

"I'm glad you like it."

I worked hard for this car. Really hard. I normally don't splurge on things like this, but I'd wanted a BMW for as long as I could remember. I figured I worked hard enough for my money, so I should enjoy it. Plus, I made some really good investment choices a year or so after we opened the restaurant. I've already got the top down. She starts to braid her hair in a long braid, and pulls it so it rests over her left shoulder. I track every movement as I put my seat belt on. She puts on some sunglasses she pulled out of her bag, and buckles her seat belt. She looks over at me with a face splitting grin. "Let's go! I'm ready."

I mimic her grin and pull out onto the street. "Don't you want to know where we're going?"

She shakes her head. "Nope. I love surprises." Noted.

I gun it as soon as we get onto a major highway outside of the city. I look over to see her reaction hoping I haven't pushed her too far. I can get carried away sometimes. She lets out a "Whoop!" and throws her hands up in the air. Obviously that makes me go faster. She throws her head back and laughs. This right here will be what I remember in eleven days.

I take her on a tour of the outskirts of the city before I circle back around to downtown. I feel like a teenager who doesn't know how to act on a first date. Rosa keeps pulling at the hem of her shorts. I guess we're both nervous. I pull into a parking spot downtown, and put the car in park. "Ready for your first surprise?"

She unbuckles her seat belt and jumps from the car before I can even put the top back up. When I open my car door she's standing there waiting on me. "Impatient much?" I jokingly say as I start walking down the sidewalk.

"I just want to see where you've brought me so bad!" She unbraids her hair as we walk. I almost walk face first into a light pole because I can't take my eyes off this woman. I better watch where I'm walking or I'll walk out into traffic.

We round the corner and she gasps. "The market? I went to a market last weekend with Juli, but she didn't bring me here. This one is huge!"

"This is the market for local vendors. You have to have a pass to get in. Come on." I reach out to grab her hand so I can intertwine our fingers, and I realize our hands fit perfectly together. I pull her in the direction of the entrance. My face is hurting from smiling so much.

"So this is where you buy all your food?"

"Yep," I answer, stopping to show my pass to an employee, as we walk through the small tent that serves as an entrance. "Sometimes I come down to see if they have anything new. Sometimes I have to send my sous chef though. Depends how busy things are."

We walk by a newer vendor that sells handmade pasta. I let go of her hand so she can get her phone out and snap a few photos of his display. "Did you ever start your blog?"

"I did actually. I've gained around a hundred followers so far."

"That's great!"

"It is. I wish I could gain traction like that with my article for Foodie though." She sighs as she stows her phone in her back pocket. "I just feel lost when it comes to the article to be honest. I keep rewriting parts of it."

"What if you wrote your article the way you write your blog?"

She completely stops walking in the middle of the aisle. "I hadn't thought about that." She resumes walking, but slower than before. "That's not what they are expecting though. I applied with a portfolio that doesn't match how I prefer to write. But now when I write in the style that got me the job, I don't feel like myself."

"Maybe you should write two? One in your old style and one in your new style. Let them decide what they want."

She stops walking and looks up at me. She nods her head and smiles. "That's a great idea!" She grabs both my hands in hers and squeezes. As corny as it may be, my heart feels like it skips a beat. "Thank you! You've been such a big help throughout this process. I don't know what I would have done if you hadn't agreed to help me."

I give her hands a little squeeze back. "It's been my pleasure." That's an understatement.

She keeps a hold of one of my hands as we keep walking through all the booths. I introduce her to a few of my friends, and she takes photos of the displays as we go. I think my friends like her better than they like me, and I can't blame them.

We stop at a few booths to buy some supplies for one of her surprises later. I gather up our bags and take hold of her hand once again, directing us through the thinning crowd to a nearby booth that's overflowing with lemons. "Do I get to know the story now?"

She smiles as a blush sweeps across her face, "I have no idea what you're talking about."

We browse the stand, searching for the perfect lemons for later. I can tell she's trying not to look at me, embarrassment written all over her face. I lean my back against the stand so I can look at her, careful not to disturb the display. "Oh, I think you do."

She turns to face me, trying to keep a smile from forming on her face. "It was just a silly dare in college. Not a big deal. A few other girls skinny dipped with me. There, you know the story. Now, answer my question. What's your biggest fear?"

I move closer to her so I can grab the lemons from her hand. Our fingers touch for the briefest of moments and I choose to linger there for a moment longer than necessary. "Losing someone I love. What's the top item on your bucket list?"

I pay as she speaks, quieter than before. "I want to visit all seven continents. What was your first impression of me when we first met?"

I grab her hand and gently pull her out into the main walkway so we can start walking back to the car. I'm silent for so long we have enough time to make it back to the car. I walk with her to the passenger side door, but neither of us make a move to get in. She leans back against the door and looks up at me with apprehension in her eyes. I crowd her against the car door as I place our bags on the ground at our feet. I reach out and set both hands on her waist, pulling her towards me. "You floored me, Rosa."

She surprises me by reaching up and grabbing the back of my neck and pulling me down for a kiss.

The moment our lips touch, I know last night wasn't a fluke. I thought maybe tensions were just high because of our situation. I've been trying to find the right time since picking her up this morning to test out my theory.

The kiss lasts only a few moments before she breaks away. She looks up at me and smiles. "I knew I didn't make it up."

I brush my thumb over her lips as I stare into her eyes. "No making that up, Rosa."

17

YOU'RE BLUSHING

Rosalie

I KNEW I DIDN'T make it up. I laid in my bed all night tossing and turning, wondering if I somehow made up my connection with Matteo.

Did we just get caught up in the heat of the moment? Was I just frightened because of the storm and I chose someone to bring me comfort? Did I actually make up the entire thing and I'm actually in a coma right now? 3 a.m. Rosalie is not fun to be around.

I was half convinced he wasn't going to show up this morning. I thought he must have gone home last night and changed his mind. Come to his senses. Realized he wants nothing to do with me. But no. He's here.

We're currently driving to the next mystery location—with the top down—listening to some awesome Italian music. I can't believe he put this much effort into this date. I was expecting to maybe walk around downtown and go to lunch, but he thought of something creative and outside-of-the-box for us to do.

He turns down the radio after the song ends. "So, what do you think?"

"He was really awesome! I can't believe you got to see him in concert. His name is Fred... what?"

He laughs, "Fred De Palma."

I grab his phone and search for my pick on his music app. "My turn!" I hit play and the main song from *The Phantom of the Opera* starts to play. I look over to gauge his reaction.

He takes his sunglasses off and hangs them on his shirt collar and grins at me. "I call dibs on Christine!" No freaking way. He starts the first line at the perfect time. He doesn't hold back, and neither do I. I know I've met my match when he starts playing imaginary instruments and finishes it all off with a horrible high note at the end. I feel like I'm getting a glimpse of the Matteo no one else gets to see, and oh man, I'm in trouble.

We're both laughing so hard we can't breathe when we pull up to a restaurant a few minutes later. He puts the car in park and turns to face me with disbelief written all over his face. "There's no way you've seen the Broadway show that many times. That must have been so expensive."

I wipe the tears from my eyes and shake my head. "My boss gets tickets all the time. She never uses them, and I'm the only one brave enough to ask for them."

"Clever. I've seen it once a few years ago, but I put the movie on for background noise a lot when I'm working." He points a finger at me with a mischievous grin on his face. "Wait right there."

He gets out of the car and comes over to open the door for me. I accept his hand as I step out of the car and curtsy. "Why thank you, sir."

He continues to hold my hand as we start walking to the front door of the restaurant. I pull my phone out and snap a few photos of the stone building. It's set back a bit from the road and is surrounded by shops and other locally owned businesses. There are five tables out front.

He pulls my seat out for me before going around the table to take a seat, then hands me a menu. "They have the best ossobuco in town. Save some room for dessert though." He gives me a wink before looking down at his own menu.

The waiter comes by and we place our order. After he leaves Matteo leans closer to me. "Show me your blog."

I shake my head. "It's not very good."

Goofy Matteo from the car is suddenly gone. "I don't believe that for a second, Rosa."

Now I'm fidgeting. I can see he's not going to back down, so I sigh and text him the link. "Fine, but don't judge me."

His face turns serious as he leans over the table. "I will never judge you, only praise you."

I suddenly can't get my lungs to cooperate. "You haven't even read it."

He leans back in his chair and pulls his phone out of his pocket. He never looks away from me. "I don't have to. I know you, Rosa." He suddenly shifts his attention to my lips. I slightly part them as I take a breath. I watch as his eyes darken and he shifts in his seat. "Watch yourself, Rosa."

I squirm in my seat again. I can't help it. Matteo is lighting my entire body on fire. He leans forward again and rests his elbows on the table.

"Are you thinking about what it felt like to have my lips on you? Tasting you?"

I nod my head slowly without breaking eye contact. "Yes."

He leans back and smiles just as the waiter arrives with our salads and bread. "Good."

I have to squeeze my legs together to give myself some much needed relief. When the waiter walks away, Matteo leans in to whisper, "You're blushing." He pulls away with a smirk on his face.

He unlocks his phone and starts reading my blog. The expression on his face never changes. When he gets done he sets his phone down and looks up at me. "Do the marketing for my restaurant."

I pause with a fork full of salad halfway to my mouth. "What?"

"I want you to do the marketing for the ten year anniversary of the restaurant. I want you to take the photos and write for my new website, and I want to use your photos for artwork in the main room."

I can't believe he would hire me just from looking at my blog. He picks up his phone, unlocks it, finds what he is looking for, and hands it to me. "How much for this photo?" The photo he helped me take of the rose and the mountains in the background is on the screen.

"You want to buy that?"

He nods his head. "Yes. How much?"

I'm shaking my head as I had his phone back to him. "I can't ask you to pay for that. You've driven me around for the past week and taken so much time out of your schedule. I'll give it to you. Consider it a thank you gift."

He sighs and accepts defeat. "Fine. I accept your thank you gift." Before he picks his fork back up he looks me in the eye with such determination I can feel it coming off him in waves. "Your blog is excellent. Don't ever let anyone tell you any differently."

"Oh, let me guess, you'll beat them up for me?" I laugh as he sets his fork down and gives me a look that could set the room on fire.

"No, Rosa. I'll find them and lay them at your feet so you can use them as a stepping stone on your way to greatness."

My breath is coming in short pants as I take in this man in front of me. I've never had someone believe in me like this. Not since my father.

Matteo gestures to my plate. "Eat up. We've got another stop after this, and I don't want us to be late."

Matteo pulls on my hand to stop me. We've been walking for a few minutes since we left the restaurant. "Okay, close your eyes."

I laugh as we move to the side of the walkway so we aren't in anyone's way. "How will I navigate if my eyes are closed?"

"I'll help you. Don't worry." He smiles as he extends his hand to me. "Trust me?"

I grin and close my eyes as I take his hand. He puts one arm around my waist and pulls me close to him.

I can somewhat make out the direction changes as we walk. We take a left, then a right, and we cross a street after that. He pulls me to a stop and leans down to whisper in my ear. "Don't move." That sends chills down my arms. I hear a bell that normally indicates the opening of a shop door, then his arm is back around me. I jump slightly because I wasn't expecting it. He chuckles. "Relax. It's just me."

We move forward a few more steps before he picks me up. I make a little yelp sound and he sets me back down. The air is a little cooler now. "Sorry. I should have warned you. There were a few stairs to go up." He directs me through a few more twists and turns before we come to a stop. I haven't heard any voices, so I'm assuming we are alone. He lets go of me and moves away. "Okay, you can open your eyes."

I open them and squint from the bright lights in the room. I look around and see... machinery? What the hell?

I look back at him and he's grinning, he gestures around the room. "This is a gelato shop, and this is where they make all their gelato."

I return his grin and start walking around the room to investigate. "So we get to go on a tour?"

He shakes his head. "No. We get to make some gelato to take home for dessert tonight."

My smile gets even bigger and I do a little shimmy. "No way!"

He nods his head. "What flavor do you want to make? They have some we can try in this freezer." He walks over to a large freezer and opens the door. There have to be at least thirty different flavors for us to try.

I float over to the freezer with wide eyes. "Holy shit."

Matteo presses in closer behind me to get a good look. "This is my friend Gino's shop. I told him you loved trying new flavors of ice cream and I wanted you to try some authentic gelato. He went a little overboard with the selection."

"Are you kidding? This is amazing!" I turn and throw my arms around his neck. He doesn't hesitate to pull me close.

"I'm glad you like it. Now let's get to work. We'll have to come back later and pick it up after it's done. Once we put it in one of these machines it takes a couple hours or so to finish."

We pull away from the hug to get to work. This is going to be fun.

18

MINE TO KEEP

Matteo

THE LOOK ON ROSA'S face as she whisks the gelato makes the favor I owe Gino worth it. She picked the stracciatella flavor which just happens to be my favorite. It's kind of like a creamy chocolate chip flavor.

I can't help but laugh as I watch her struggle to lift the mixing bowl so we can pour the mixture into the gelato machine. I take a step in her direction and take the bowl from her and place it under one arm and hold the spatula out to her with my free hand.

"Why don't I hold it and you can scrape it all off the sides?"

She rolls her eyes and takes the spatula with a grin on her face. "Fine. I could do it on my own, you know?"

I look at her and laugh as we both walk toward the gelato machine. "Oh I have no doubt." I may or may not have added a sarcastic note to my voice just because I like messing with her.

She playfully whacks me with the spatula on the arm. "I could! Here, give it back. I can carry it across the room just as well as you can."

I laugh and lift the bowl above my head so it's well out of her reach. "Oh no. You had your chance." She pushes up onto her tip toes and pushes her chest up against mine to try and reach the bowl. She's basically climbing me. Now I'm definitely not giving it up. "I can play this game all day, Rosa."

She does a little jump to try and gain some height. That only causes her to rub her body down mine on the way down. My cock jumps to attention. I place the bowl on top of the freezer and have Rosa in my arms before she can even register what's happening.

She squeals but doesn't put up a fight as I spin her and push her up against the freezer door. The smile on her face morphs into fire in her eyes.

I can feel every curve of her body. I have one hand supporting her weight while my other snakes around the back of her neck.

We're silent as we take each other in. This is the first time I've given myself the opportunity to really look at her this close. Her dark lashes cast shadows along her cheek bones as she blinks at me with the most beautiful eyes. I hadn't noticed the little freckles on her cheeks before, or the tiny scar above her right eyebrow. I reach up and trace it. Her eyes close and her breathing becomes heavy as I continue to take her in. I can practically see the wheels turning in her brain. "What are you thinking about, Rosa?"

She tightens her legs around me and opens her eyes to stare into my very soul. "How much I want you."

I tighten my hold on her and kiss her. I kiss her like she's mine to kiss. Mine to take. Mine to keep. She runs her fingers through my hair as she deepens the kiss. A kiss with this woman is better than sex with anyone else.

I know she can feel the effect she has on me. My cock is straining at my zipper so hard it hurts. I need this woman like I need my next breath. I leave her lips and start kissing a path down her neck. She leans her head to the side to give me better access. She's breathing hard, making her chest rise and fall rapidly. I continue my path until I reach the exposed cleavage I haven't been able to stop looking at all day.

As soon as I start to trail my hand down her gorgeous body I hear the front door open and Gino calls out to us. I groan as I set Rosa back down on her feet. She readjusts her top and fans her face. I don't think that'll help much. She looks like she's been thoroughly fucked. I'm actually glad Gino put a stop to our shenanigans. I do not want our first time to be against a freezer in Gino's shop. Rosa deserves better than that.

I turn my back to the door to readjust myself in my pants as Gino walks in. "Ah Matteo." I turn and embrace my old friend. "I hope you found the shop to your liking. I made sure my assistant had everything prepared this morning."

I pull away from the hug and give him a slap on the back a little harder than I normally would. That's for cock-blocking me. "Everything was perfect. Thanks for doing this on such short notice. Rosa, This is my friend from culinary school, Gino. Gino, this is Rosalie. The woman I was telling you about."

She steps forward and extends her hand. "It's nice to meet you. Thank you for letting us take over your shop today."

Gino takes her hand and kisses it. That fucker. "The pleasure is all mine, bella."

I take a step toward them and place my arm around Rosa's waist. Gino lets go of her and looks up at me with a shit eating grin and pure mischief written all over his face. That double fucker. Rosa sinks into my side and my heartbeat starts to return to a normal level. What the hell is wrong with me?

He takes a step back and begins rolling up his shirt sleeves and washes his hands. "I thought I would stop by and get the machine going. Since this is such a small batch you can come by later tonight and pick it up." He dries his hands and turns to look around the room. "Where's the mixture?"

He looks at me and I point to the top of the freezer. He goes over and pulls it down. He gives me a puzzling look. I hold my hands up. "Don't ask. How's the new baby? Gia recovering well?"

A beaming smile takes over his face as he begins moving around the room. "Baby Amara is amazing. Gia is doing okay. She's over the moon of course, but the recovery has been hard on her."

"Fatherhood looks good on you." I rub the back of my neck. "I'm sorry you had to leave Gia to come out like this today. I didn't think about that."

He shakes his head as he pushes a few buttons on the gelato machine. "Don't be. Gia and her mom needed some time alone with the baby. Her mom will only be here for a few weeks, so I'm glad they get some girl time."

I find myself absently playing with the ends of Rosa's hair. "Who would have thought you'd be the first one out of all of us to get married and have a kid?" I turn to Rosa and gesture at Gino. "He was the wild one of the bunch in culinary school. Always getting the rest of us in trouble."

She laughs as Gino walks toward us with his hands up. "Hold up. That's not how I remember it at all." He cups his hand to shield his mouth from me and stage whispers to Rosa, "I seem to recall a certain someone convincing us all to go cliff jumping after graduation."

I roll my eyes. I'll never live this story down. "It's not like I forced you into it or anything."

Rosa laughs as she looks between Gino and I. "What's so bad about cliff diving?"

Gino leans his elbows on the counter and leans forward slightly. "Turns out the place Matteo took us has a very clear no cliff diving policy. And for good reason, Roberto almost broke his leg that night."

I run my fingers through my hair. "It's not like I pushed him. He just didn't listen to our advice on where to jump."

Rosa smiles up at me, the remnants of laughter on her face. "I knew you were a trouble maker."

I lean down and kiss her on the nose, before I start leading her toward the door. I'm not going to give Gino another chance to talk about any other embarrassing stories. "Do you need anything else from us?"

He shakes his head. "Nope. You're good to go. I'll text you when it's done so you can come pick it up, or I can bring it to your place on my way home. Just let me know."

Rosa turns to Gino as I pull her out the door to the kitchen. "Thanks again!"

I can barely hear him say goodbye as we walk out onto the street. I slow our pace now that we're alone. Rosa situates her sunglasses with her free hand as she looks around the street. "This is a beautiful area. I didn't get to see it before since I had to keep my eyes closed."

I pull her across me and slip over to the other side of her so I'm on the street side of the road. She gives me a smile as we join hands once again. "This is actually where I live. Right up there actually." I point to a four story stone building a few hundred feet ahead of us. "We just need to stop by the car and get our dinner supplies before we go up."

She stops walking and pulls on my hand to make me stand in front of her. She looks so excited. "You're cooking what we bought at the market for dinner?"

I shake my head no and her face falls. I reach down and gently pull her chin up so she's looking at me. "We're cooking what we bought at the market for dinner."

"No way!" She pulls me so hard toward my condo I almost lose my balance and face plant. "Hurry up! This is going to be so fun! What are we making?"

I shake my head and smile even though she can't see me. "That's another surprise. You're going to have to wait and see." I don't know when I turned into the guy that plans dates like this, but after I left Alda's last night I knew exactly how I wanted to spend my first date with Rosa. I just hope I can pull it off. I've never cooked something like this before.

She squeals again. I can't believe how much I like that noise. "I can't wait. Teach me everything!"

She suddenly comes to a dead stop. I was wondering how long it would take her to realize she has no idea where the car is from here. She turns around and looks at me. She puts her hand over her mouth trying to hold back a laugh. "I guess I'm a little lost."

"Let me show you the way." I pull her down a side street to start walking toward the car.

It takes a few turns to make it to my usual parking spot. I let go of her hand and pop the trunk. She comes up next to me and grabs a few bags. I gather the rest in one arm and close the trunk. We start walking to the condo I've had for five years now. It's within walking distance to the restaurant, and the few friends I keep up with all live nearby.

I spent an hour last night making sure everything was clean so Rosa wouldn't find any dirty clothes laying around when she came over tonight. I never bring girls back to my place, so I'm suddenly feeling very nervous. What if she hates my place?

What if it freaks her out to be alone with me at my place? I know we've been getting closer, but this takes things to an entirely new level. Maybe I should have asked her if she was okay with this?

I open the front door of the building for her and direct her to the stairs.

What if I like the way she looks in my place too much? This can't last. I can't get attached.

Too late.

19

LET ME IN

Rosalie

MY HEART IS IN my throat as we walk up the four flights of stairs.

I can't believe how nervous I am. I've had dinner with Matteo almost every night for the past week. Why am I getting nervous now? Who am I kidding? We both know this isn't just dinner. This is everything. At least to me anyway. This has been one of the best days I've had since coming to Italy, and my time in Italy has been the best I've had since my father passed.

I miss him. I miss the memories we could have made. I miss the advice he would have given.

Matteo stops in front of the door to condo number twelve which brings my thoughts back to reality. He shifts his bags to one arm to dig his key out of his pocket. He unlocks the door and steps inside. There's no need to turn on a light. The natural lighting coming in through the large windows brighten up the room beautifully. The condo is exactly as I expected. Modern but warm. Minimal but stylish.

I can see the large kitchen to the right with bar stools around the island. The smaller living area to the left holds a large dark brown leather couch and a coffee table with magazines spread out on top. There's a hallway in the middle of the two. We both set our bags down on the kitchen island. Matteo leans against the counter and crosses his arms as he watches me take in his space.

"Would you like a tour?"

I nod my head. "I would like that very much."

"Good." He leads me into the main living area. He turns and motions toward the kitchen. "As you can imagine, this space looked very different when I bought this place. I basically remodeled the entire living area and kitchen. I also did some work in the bathroom, but everything else is original."

He lets go of my hand so I can explore the kitchen on my own. "I bet you spend most of your time in here."

"Yes. That's why it takes up most of the living area. Cooking is like an escape for me. It's the way I relax."

I turn back to look at the living area. "So no TV then?"

"I wouldn't say that. I like to watch movies every now and then." He walks over to the coffee table and pulls up on the edge. The table top lifts up to be the perfect height to sit on the couch and eat.

There's also plenty of storage under the table top. I can see a few card games and more magazines poking out. Matteo grabs a remote and presses a few buttons. A screen directly across from the couch starts to come down and a projector turns on overhead.

I walk over and sit on the couch. "How did I miss that before?"

"I like to keep the electronics hidden away. Want to see the bedroom?" He wiggles his eyebrows at me as I stand from the couch. I can't help but laugh as we walk down the hallway until we reach the last door.

He opens it to reveal a king sized bed with black bedding and a nightstand on either side. There's a large dresser on the right with a mirror above it. There is also a door that I assume leads to the bathroom along the same wall. On the left are more beautiful windows that showcase the view of the street.

He walks in and opens his arms to motion around the room. "It's not very big, but I spend most of my time in the kitchen and living area anyway."

"I'm pretty sure your bedroom is the size of my apartment in New York. This is like a mansion to me." I'm in awe as I take in the photograph of the Italian coast on the wall above his bed. "It's beautiful."

He walks over so he's standing behind me. My breath catches in my throat. He's so close. I could lean back only an inch and make contact. "I took that during one of my trips to the Amalfi Coast."

The scene looks so similar to photos of southern France. I feel a pain in my chest that I so often try to forget, try to push away. This time though, I let myself feel the loss of a father, of a friend. I'm facing away from Matteo, so he can't see the look of anguish I am trying—and failing—to keep off my face.

I can hear him start in the direction of the kitchen. "Would you like to make some lemonade with the lemons from the market?"

I use the brief solitude to pull myself together as best I can before replying, "That sounds wonderful." As soon as I round the corner to the kitchen Matteo stops in his tracks. He abandons his work at the kitchen counter and comes over to me.

He places both of his hands on either side of my face. "What's wrong, Rosa?"

The compassion in his eyes continues to break down my walls. Tears start to flow down my face. The feeling of crying in front of someone is so foreign that I can't even think of the words to say. Matteo's face is full of desperation. "Let me in, Rosa."

I open my mouth, but no words form. He releases my face and takes one of my hands to pull me toward the back of the room. There's a door to a terrace I hadn't noticed before. He opens the door and leads me to a table and two chairs outside. He pulls out a chair for me, and sits in the other.

I take in the view for a moment. He doesn't rush me or push me to talk in any way. The tears have stopped flowing enough for me to speak. "Since I've been in Italy, I've been thinking about my dad so much. He used to have a flat like this when he was in college. He would bring out his old photo album and show me photos of his life in France."

I pause for a moment and push my hair behind my ears. "I guess being here has just brought up a lot of memories. And then there was the storm from the other night. It's been so long since I've had a freak out like that. My mom paid a lot of money for therapy sessions after my father passed." I roll my eyes, thinking about what my mom would say if she saw me the other night. "She would be so disappointed to hear all her money was wasted."

I can feel another round of tears forming in my eyes as I think back about my time spent with my dad, and of the time I could have also spent with my mom. "My mom never took much of an interest in me. She was always so focused on her job, or spending time with her friends. My dad was the only real parent I ever had."

Matteo hasn't moved a muscle. He just sits there and listens as I pour my heart out to him. I feel another tear break free and fall down my cheek. Matteo is suddenly bent down in front of me. I didn't even hear him get up. He catches the tear with his thumb and pushes my chin up so I'm making eye contact with him. When he looks at me like this I feel like he is stripping me bare. Like he can see every flaw I'll ever have. Like he can see me. He still doesn't say anything; he just holds my hand.

"I feel closer to my dad than I have in years since coming to Italy. This is who my dad was." I motion around me with my free hand. "He was light and love. He loved trying new foods and going to new places just as much as he loved the sea."

Matteo catches another tear as it falls down my face. "Can I take you out on my sailboat tomorrow?"

I feel my heart rate pick up. I've not been on a boat since that day, but I can't let this chance pass me by. I smile up at him as I use the back of my hand to wipe the moisture off my face. "I would love that."

He smiles at me and I feel the smile all the way to my toes.

20

Mesmerizing

Matteo

We sit in silence as I watch every move she makes. She's an enchantress, and I am her willing victim. She has no idea what she does to me. I watch as she takes a drink. As she watches the birds fly overhead. As she steals every last fiber of restraint I have. It took one tear to bring me to my knees. One tear and I crumbled in her hands.

It's been over an hour since she broke down. I've never seen such beautiful raw emotion. The love she has for her father mimicking the love I have for mine.

I hated to see her cry, but I loved seeing that side of her. The vulnerability. The trust.

She tucks her hair behind her ear and looks over at me. She gives me a little smile that I'm pretty sure is reserved just for me. "I love it here." She breaks eye contact and looks back over the city. I'm on the top floor of one of the tallest buildings in this area of town, so the view is pretty nice.

She stands to look over the edge of the balcony. She leans over the railing, giving me a perfect view of her from behind. I stand so quickly I startle her. I turn and walk back into the living room before I take her on the balcony. "We... uh... better get started on dinner." I sound like a blubbering idiot.

I readjust myself in my pants as I walk into the kitchen. Dinner. Right. Focus.

I start unloading the bags from the market as she walks into the kitchen. She comes over to help me unload the rest of the bags while I start rinsing the vegetables. "What can I help with?"

Just the sound of her voice makes me have to readjust myself again. How on earth am I going to make it through this dinner? I clear my throat. "You can start by chopping the vegetables." I put all the vegetables I just washed in a bowl and hand it to her. I grab a knife from the rack and hand that to her as well.

I have to calm down or I won't be able to control myself. I need to wait. She's too special. She deserves more than me taking her on the dining table. I don't want to fuck this up. I've managed to control myself this far, surely I can make it through dinner so I can make this experience special for her.

"What are we making?"

I gather the seasoning we needed and place everything on the kitchen island. "Well, the dish doesn't actually have a name. It's traditionally a soup from the Tuscany region that features vegetables and beans. It's traditionally served with bread. We're going to put our own spin on it by thickening up the soup base, serving it in a bread bowl, and adding bacon."

Her face lights up. "Bacon is my favorite!"

The twenty questions game worked in my favor. "This is one of the dishes I've been trying out to hopefully put on the menu at the new restaurant. It's kind of like a modern version of ribollita. With the new restaurant I want to take old dishes, unpopular dishes, and classic dishes and put my own spin on them. There's some dishes that only older generations like, and some that haven't been popular for a while. I want to bring new life to them."

Talking about my plans for the new restaurant has calmed my cock down a bit. Thank fuck.

She gives me a beaming smile that I feel all the way to the tip of my toes. "That's a really good idea. It'll be like you're bringing all the generations together."

"I've got a problem though. That's as far as my ideas have gotten so far. That's not enough to open a new restaurant with. I've just got ideas. For the past few months I've been trying to figure out a way to make them happen."

She pauses and looks up at me. I hadn't even realized I was watching her. "I would eat there. That has to mean something. I work for Foodie magazine after all! What was it you told me? Don't give up on your dream, even if it means finding a new dream. Seems to me like you've found your dream. Go for it. You'll figure out all the details."

She looks back down and resumes chopping like she didn't just give me the biggest confidence boost of my life. I can't keep the smile off my face, partly because of the bomb she just dropped and because of the way she's struggling to chop the vegetables. I cross my arms and lean back against the counter to watch her. "For such a foodie, you sure are struggling over there."

She laughs and puts down the knife so she can put her hands on her hips. "I never said I could cook! I'm good at eating the food, not making it." I take a step toward her and her eyes go big. She snatches the knife from the cutting board so she can hold it hostage. "No. I'm going to finish this. I promise I can do it."

I don't say a word as I come to her and spin her so she's facing the counter. I step behind her and push my hips up against hers. Her breath catches as I push her hair to the side and run my nose along the side of her neck. I run one hand down from her neck to take control of her hand that's holding the knife. "I know you can do it, Rosa.

Let me show you the proper technique so you don't cut yourself."

I take her other hand and show her how to position it. Then I show her how to move the knife. After she gets a good rhythm going, I let go. "There. Now you're a pro." I walk back around to the stove and situate myself in my pants once again. This woman.

I take one last glance at her before I begin working on the bacon. I prepared the soup base before I left this morning so the flavor would be just right for tonight. All that's left to do is prepare the bacon and the vegetables. That shouldn't take us more than thirty minutes or so.

One look at her face and I can see she is concentrating on what she's doing. "What do you want the name of your new restaurant to be?"

I turn the stove on to begin warming up before I walk to the fridge to retrieve the soup base and the bacon. "I don't know to be honest."

She never looks up from the cutting board as she speaks. "So it won't be Moretti's?"

I shake my head and laugh. "No. This restaurant will be mine. I want my dad's input and his support, but I want to be the one making all the decisions." The soup base starts to warm up as I slice the bacon. My hands feel like they are on autopilot from the years of similar motions.

I glance over my shoulder to check on her. She has al-most all the vegetables cut in the time it took me to put everything on the stove. I go over to the island and lean on my forearms to get a better look. I expected to see junior chef level work, but I am pleasantly surprised. "You're a natural."

My new favorite shade of pink takes over her cheeks. "I enjoy knitting sometimes, so I guess that means I'm good with my hands." She lays her knife down and looks up at me expectantly. "Now what can I do?"

I push away from the counter to check on the stove. After taking inventory of what's left to be done I give her a few options. "Do you want to cut the holes in the bread to make bowls or do you want to tend to the bacon and vegetables?"

She gets another big smile on her face. "Bacon. Definitely bacon."

I smile as I step to the side to make room for her in front of the stove. She steps in front of me and begins inspecting her new work station. I hand her a wooden spatula. "You can use the spatula to scrape the vegetables into the pan with the bacon. We'll transfer everything in with the soup base after it's all cooked."

She gently slides the vegetables into the pan and begins stirring them all together. I come up behind her closer than is necessary. "Do you want me to show you how to flip a skillet?"

Confusion takes over her face. "Why would I flip it?"

I shake my head and laugh. "Not flip it over. That's what we call this." I take the pan and quickly move it back and forth on the stove. This causes the contents to be suspended midair and land softly back in the pan. "This is the most effective way to stir and keep the food from burning on the bottom.

Another smile lights up her face. "Can I try?"

I nod my head as I hand the pan back over. "Just be careful not to lift the skillet up off the stove. That could cause food to fly everywhere."

She moves timidly at first, then slowly gains more confidence until she finally gets her first flip. She lets go of the pan and does a victory dance while shouting, "I did it!"

I can't contain the smile on my face. "You did so well, Rosa."

21

Not a Chance in Hell

Matteo

She sets the table as I plate our food, then she sits and I place her plate in front of her. She watches intensely as I take my seat and pick up my fork. I can't help but notice she doesn't get her phone out like normal. "No photos of the food tonight?"

She shakes her head, a smile on her face. "No. This one is just for me." She finally breaks eye contact to try her food. She moans when she takes her first bite and I clinch the fork in my hand and close my eyes to keep from exploding in my pants. Oblivious to my discomfort she says, "This is amazing! I could write an entire spread for food like this!"

I open my eyes to look at her with a beaming smile on my face. "I'm glad you like it." I don't know when her opinion became so important to me, but it definitely is.

She pinches off a small piece of bread so she can dip it into the soup. After she plops it in her mouth, she looks up to catch me watching her. Another blush creeps across her face. "You're staring."

I nod my head. "I am."

She tilts her head to the side. "Why?"

"Because you're mesmerizing."

She averts her gaze and begins running the tip of her index finger along the edge of her plate. "I'm not that interesting."

I lean forward in my seat. "You couldn't be more wrong about that, Rosa." I reach across the small table to lift her chin. Uncertainty takes over her face. "If I had to choose between watching the sunset alone or watching paint dry with you, I'd pick you every time."

A smile spreads across her face. "You can't mean that. Watching paint dry would suck." We both laugh as I release her chin. "At my first job, my manager told me to sit and watch the paint dry on a bench in Times Square. He said he was so tired of people ignoring the wet paint signs."

I quirk my head to the side. "Are you serious?"

A shakes her head. "Not at all."

I lean back in my seat as she bursts out laughing. I point at her with my fork, a smile planted firmly on my face. "You are scary good at that. You could have fooled me."

She wipes a tear from her eye from the laughter. "You should have seen your face."

Still smiling, I say, "Did you go to acting school or something?"

She shakes her head. "No. I took a drama class as an elective in college."

"I think you missed your calling, Rosa."

She pushes her hair over her shoulder to keep it from dragging across her plate while she eats. "You were so young when you graduated from culinary school. Do you feel like you missed out on the typical college experience?"

I wait until my mouth isn't full to answer. "No. I made some amazing friends that I still keep in contact with. We kind of continued hanging out after we graduated. The only real difference is we had jobs instead of going to class all the time. That all changed as we got older."

She dabs her mouth with a napkin before she says, "In what way?"

I let out a deep breath. "We all grew up I guess. That means different things for different people." I lean my elbows against the table as I speak. "Gino for instance. He met his wife not long after we graduated. It took him a few years to pop the question, but they've been married for a while now. A few of my other friends decided to travel for a while after they saved up enough cash."

"What about you?"

I shrug. "I wanted to open my own restaurant. Granted, I had to open my first restaurant with my dad. Funds were a bit low then." I smile to myself, thinking back about my dad and I working our asses off to succeed. "I like working with him. I just wish I could make more of the choices. You know?"

She leans forward, her hands resting on the table, watching me intently. "I get it. Maybe your dad just needs to see how capable you are. It's hard to see things when they are right under your nose sometimes."

I nod, a smile forming on my face. "What about you? What do you want?" She opens her mouth, but I raise my hand to cut her off. "Other than the job at Foodie."

She fidgets as she uncrosses her legs only to recross them again. "I've never really thought about that to be honest. My focus has mainly been on work."

"I understand that. My dad thinks I should focus more on living instead of working."

She nods her head as she leans back in her chair. "I don't even know what my life would be like without my job."

"Do you like your job?"

Her smile takes my breath away. "I like that it brought me here."

I can't help but smile back at her. "Me too."

She looks down at her now empty plate. "Can I help with the dishes?"

I look down at my own plate to find it empty. I hadn't even realized we had finished our meal. When I'm with Rosa I find myself losing time, like the concept of time no longer exists.

I push my chair back and stand. "I'll wash, if you dry."

She smiles up at me again. "Deal."

We take our dishes to the kitchen. Neither of us says a word. I'm aware of every move she makes. Every light touch setting me on fire.

I rinse the last dish and hand it to her. I dry my hands and we turn to face each other. Both of us are breathing heavy. I take a step toward her and push her hair behind one ear. She closes her eyes as I trace the small scar above her eyebrow. I trace her jaw line, down her neck, and back up to her lips.

"Rosa?" She opens her eyes to look at me while I continue my exploration of her beautiful face. "I need you to tell me what you want, Rosa."

She takes a deep breath. "You. I want you." Our lips collide as I pick her up and place her on the counter. She spreads her legs and I step in between them. She closes them around me as I tangle my hands in her hair. I trail my hands down until they are at the hem of her shirt. I only break our kiss for a moment as I lift her shirt over her head. My shirt follows shortly after. "I need to be in you, Rosa." I pick her up and she wraps her arms around my neck and her legs around my waist. We don't break the kiss as I carry her into my bedroom. I set her down on the edge of my bed and step back to look at her. Her chest is heaving and her hair is spread out all around her. There is fire in her eyes. "Take your clothes off, Rosa. I want to see you."

I take a step back so I can take her all in while she sheds her clothes. She keeps eye contact with me as she stands and unzips her shorts. She pushes them down her thighs and when they fall to the ground, she steps out of them, kicking them to the side. She slowly reaches back and unclips her bra, adding it to the pile of discarded clothes. I feel every muscle in my body tense as she hooks her thumbs in her panties and slowly takes them off.

I give myself a moment to take in her beautiful body before my eyes find hers.

She looks down to watch as I start to undo my belt buckle. I unbutton my pants, and push them down with my boxers, kicking them towards the pile of clothes before I walk towards her.

"Beautiful. My enchantress." I need to kiss her. She's my oxygen, my tether, my Rosa. My beautiful rose. A smile spreads on my face and I reach out to grab the back of her neck. "Tell me if you want me to stop, Rosa."

She shakes her head. "Not a chance in hell."

"I'll try to be gentle."

She smiles back at me. "I don't want you to be gentle."

I break eye contact as I run my hand down her neck all the way to her hip. I run my finger over the little indention above her hip bone and move my hand so my palm is covering the center of her stomach just below her belly button. Her breath catches as I slowly move my hand down. I slip my fingers between her wet folds and her knees buckle. I catch her and pick her up so I can place her back on the bed.

"You're already so wet for me, Rosa." I climb up on the bed so I'm hovering over her. I grab her ankle and run my hand all the way up her leg until I reach the inside of her thigh. I dip my fingers between her wet folds again to find her dripping. I'm hard as steel as I push a finger inside her. Heaven. She fists the sheets as she squirms below me.

I pull out my finger so I can find her sensitive nub. I rub her in slow circles as I lower myself so I can taste her. I run my tongue along her slit and she bucks her hips up off the bed. I reach one hand up to push down just below her belly button. I bring my other hand up and push two fingers in her as I continue my assault with my tongue.

She reaches down to grab a handful of my hair. "Fuck yes."

I don't let up until she clamps her legs around my head and starts to scream my name. The best sound I've ever heard. I sit up and grab a condom from my night stand. "I need to be in you, Rosa."

"Yes. Don't hold back."

She watches as I roll the condom on and align myself at her entrance. I push in slowly inch by inch.

Every muscle in my body is shaking as I try to control myself and give her time to adjust to me. Being in this woman is like seeing a rainbow after a hurricane. Like finding water after being stranded in a desert. Like coming home.

22

YOUR TRUE NORTH

Rosalie

I CURL MY TOES as he pushes into me. I've never felt so full. I've never felt so whole.

I gasp as he bottoms out and he lowers his forehead to mine. His entire body is shaking. "Are you okay?"

I can barely find the words to answer. I nod my head. "I need you to move."

He starts to slowly move in and out. He sets a slow rhythm before he sits up and pulls my hips up from the bed to hit a new spot that makes me see stars.

We start to move together as he sets a faster and faster pace. He reaches down and strokes my clit. His rhythm grows erratic, and we scream our release together. My vision turns white as my release overtakes me.

We're both shaking as he reaches up to grab the back of my neck. He kisses me before pulling out. He climbs off the bed and points at me as he walks toward the bathroom. "Don't move."

Now that's funny. "I don't think I could even if I wanted to."

I can hear him laugh from the bathroom before the sink turns on. I grab a pillow and hug it to my chest. I let his leather and sandalwood scent envelope me. He comes back with a washcloth and gently spreads my legs and begins to clean me. "You don't have to do this."

He doesn't hesitate. "I know." He looks up at me. "I want to." He kisses me on the forehead before taking the washcloth back to the bathroom.

When he comes back he slides in bed next to me and pulls me onto his chest so he can trace small circles on my back. We're silent for a moment as I trace his tattoo. A compass is the main focal point with rope in a design around it, and a map in the background. The design takes up most of his upper chest. What's so strange is north is at the bottom of the compass like it's pointing directly at his heart. "What does your tattoo mean?"

He takes a deep breath. "I have a sailboat that I like to take out every now and then. My grandfather bought it right before my dad moved to the States. My dad never cared for sailing, so when my grandfather passed the boat was left to me. My grandfather taught me how to use a compass to navigate, how to tie all the ropes for the sails, and how to use a map instead of just a GPS. I guess you can say that's my way of keeping his memory alive."

I push up on my elbow so I can examine it further. "Why is the compass upside down?"

"My grandfather used to say, 'The expected way isn't always the best way. You need to go to your true north.' I guess that just always stuck with me."

I take a deep breath and look up at him. His hair is all tossed about. His shoulders are relaxed. He seems content. I like him this way. He reaches up and pushes a strand of hair behind my ear. Where do we go from here? How can I move on from this in less than two weeks? "What do we do now?"

He wiggles his eyebrows and flips us so I am under him once again. He kisses a trail down my neck causing my back to arch off the bed. "We can go again."

I giggle and try to wiggle free. "You know that's not what I meant."

He sits up and looks me in the eye. He pushes a few stray hairs out of my face as he pulls me back into his lap. "What do you want from this?"

I can't answer that question. "I don't know. This is just all so new and unexpected. I still need to focus on writing my article and my blog. That's my dream." At least I think it is. I don't know anymore.

"How about this—we enjoy our time together while you're here. We don't think about what happens in two weeks. We just take it day by day. That's all we focus on because all I know is a few weeks with you is better than nothing at all. I'm not afraid to admit it, that was the best sex of my life. This has been my favorite day, well, ever. I'll take whatever you will give me, Rosa."

I swallow the lump in my throat and nod my head. "Okay."

"Okay." The doorbell startles me. Matteo jumps up and starts looking through our clothes on the floor. "That's probably Gino. He texted me earlier and said he would just bring the gelato by. I'll be right back." He pulls on his boxers and walks out the door, closing it behind him.

I get up and start gathering my clothes. What do I want from this? I have no idea. I can't come to terms with what I'm feeling. It doesn't make sense. I'm starting to feel things for Matteo that I don't understand, and I'm losing feelings for something I've loved for as long as I can remember. Writing. At least the writing I have been doing anyway.

Writing the article for Foodie seems so empty, like it doesn't represent me at all. I feel so free when I write for my blog. I feel free when I'm with Matteo too. Why has this trip changed me so much?

I finish gathering my clothes, but pull on Matteo's shirt from earlier instead. I can't stand the thought of putting my tight clothes back on. Plus, I just want to wear his shirt. It comes to my mid-thigh, so I just pull on my panties instead of my shorts.

I can hear talking in the living area, so I decide to freshen up a bit in the bathroom while I wait for Gino to leave. I splash some cold water on my face and look at myself in the mirror.

What do you want, Rosalie? What will make you happy? I thought I knew. Now, I'm not so sure.

When I walk back out into the bedroom, Matteo is waiting for me, still shirtless. He grins at me. "Shirt thief."

I laugh and motion like I'm going to pull it over my head. "Oh I'm sorry, do you want it back?"

He shakes his head as he walks toward me with fire in his eyes. "I want you to take it off, but I don't want it back." He scoops me up and kisses me. Even just a kiss with him is better than sex with anyone else.

He sets me back on the ground and breaks our kiss. I look up at him with disappointment evident on my face. He laughs and kisses my nose. "Let's eat some gelato, then we can go for round two." He grabs my hand and pulls me out of the bedroom and into the kitchen. I'm greeted with a tub full of gelato on the kitchen island.

I let go of his hand and skip over to the island so I can admire my creation. Matteo comes up behind me and gives my butt a little smack. "Don't slobber all over it." I sit down on one of the bar stools and bring my legs up under me.

"I can't help it. Have you seen my masterpiece? Perfection." I give an exaggerated chef's kiss.

He gathers two spoons and walks back over to me. "Your masterpiece?" He hands me a spoon. "If I remember correctly, you couldn't even lift the mixing bowl on your own."

"I would have done it on my own eventually, thank you very much."

He crosses his arms and laughs at me. That dick. "Oh I know you would have. The real question is how much of the mixture would have ended up on the floor?" Oh that's it.

I jump off the stool and wiggle my spoon at him. "Oh it's on mister."

He puts his hands up and starts backing away from me slowly. "No violence."

I take one step toward him and before I know it my back is pressed up against his chest. How in the world does he move that fast? I try to wiggle free. "That's not fair!"

He laughs and tightens his hold around me. "You were the one pointing a weapon at me. I had to defend myself."

I squeal when he picks me up bridal style and places me back on the stool. He pulls my spoon out of his pocket and hands it to me. I look at the spoon in disbelief. "How did you manage to put my spoon in your pocket during all that?"

He pulls out his own spoon and gathers up some gelato. "Luca makes me spar with him sometimes. The Italian Special Forces training is no joke."

I sit up straighter as I gather some gelato on my spoon. "No way! Can you teach me a few moves?"

"Sure. After you try some gelato." He holds his spoon out to me and I clink mine with his. "Cheers."

Best. Gelato. Ever. "Oh shit. That's amazing."

He smiles at me and takes another bite. "I think we make a pretty good team."

We do indeed.

23

MISS CONGENIALITY

Matteo

I'M STANDING IN BETWEEN my living room and kitchen while Rosa circles me.

"So just attack you? What if I hurt you?"

I make a point not to make eye contact with her as she completes another circle around me. "Just do it. Don't overthink it." She's quiet for a few moments before I hear a battle cry from behind me. I catch her mid-air and bring her back to my bare chest. I hold her arms against her sides and laugh as she tries her hardest to wiggle free. I bend down so I can whisper in her ear. "Maybe you should lose the battle cry, Rosa. It's a little obvious."

I release her and situate her where I was just standing. "My turn. When I grab you, I want you to use your heel to push down on the inside of my foot. Hard. Right here." I show her where I'm talking about. "Then I want you to elbow me in the stomach here." I gesture to one side of my stomach. "If that doesn't work, try to turn and knee me in

the balls. Well act like you're going to knee me in the balls."
I place both hands on her shoulders and look her in the eye.
"Don't actually knee me in the balls, Rosa."

Her eyes go wide and she nods her head. She giggles as
I start making my own circles around her. "Are you giving
me the self defense lesson from Miss Congeniality?"

"I have no idea what that means, but if that helps you
remember the moves, then sure."

She starts bouncing back and forth on her feet. "I can
do this. I can do this." She cracks her neck. "Okay, I'm..."
I don't give her a chance to finish. I grab her from behind
and bring her back to my chest. She panics and grabs at my
arms.

"You can do this, Rosa. Just think through the steps."

"Foot." She misses the important part of my foot, and
hits my big toe instead. She's barefoot, so it doesn't hurt
too bad. "Stomach." I loosen my grip when she makes
contact with my stomach. Shit that one hurt. She turns in
my arms and goes for my groin. The look of pure determination on her face makes me let go of her and place my
hands over my cock.

"Okay. Okay. That's enough."

She backs off and jumps in the air. "Yay! I did it!"

"You did good." I rub my stomach. That's going to be sore for a little while. "Has anyone ever told you, you have bony elbows?"

"You mean these babies?" She blows on her elbows like you would the barrel of a gun. "So does that mean I know Jujitsu now?"

I walk to the kitchen to grab us some water. "No. That was basic self defense. You've got to become more aware of what your body can do before you jump right into something like Jujitsu." I lean back against the counter. I toss her a water and we both take a moment to catch our breath.

She's a vision in my kitchen. Still only in my shirt, hair a mess. She's never looked more beautiful. I set my water down on the counter and walk over to her. She sets her water down and we take each other in. She breaks the silence. "Thanks for teaching me."

I trail one finger down her neck and I trace the top of my shirt. "I want you to be safe."

She swallows as I move down to trace the hem of my shirt resting on her thighs. She takes in a shuddered breath. "Am I safe with you?"

I settle my hands on either side of her face. "You'll always be safe with me." I press feather light kisses to each corner of her mouth. She wraps both arms around my neck and I lift her up so she can wrap her legs around my waist.

"What are you doing to me, Rosa?" I kiss down her neck as I lay her down on the kitchen island. "What spell have you put me under?" I push the hem of my shirt up until I can almost see her belly button. I kiss the inside of her thigh as I work my way up her delicious body. "Why do you make me feel this way? Can you feel it, Rosa? Can you feel what's between us? This pull. This need." I prop myself up on my elbows so I can look at her beautiful face. "Tell me you feel it too."

With tear filled eyes she nods her head. "I feel it, Matteo." I kiss her. I kiss her with everything I have.

I pull my shirt over her head and run my finger over her nipple. She arches her back off the counter as I dip my head down to take her other nipple in my mouth. She grinds against me. I release her just long enough to push my boxers to the ground. I go to take her panties off, but stop when I realize what I've forgotten. I go to pull away. "Need to grab a condom."

She grabs my hand while shaking her head. "I had my birth control shot before I came to Italy, and I'm clean."

I reach between her legs and pull her underwear down, and I move back into position. "I'm clean too. Are you sure this is okay?"

She nods her head. "Yes. Now come here." She grabs my chin and pulls my face down so we can resume our kiss. I reach down and run my fingers through her wet folds before I start to rub her clit. She moans into my mouth as I continue to pleasure her. "I need you in me. Now."

I position myself at her entrance and fill her in one move. She grabs my arm and hisses. I immediately stop moving and search her face. "Sorry, Rosa. Too much?"

She looks up at me and smiles. "No. Keep going." I start to move again. I set a quicker pace than our first time. I grab her around her waist and pull her closer to the edge of the counter so I can get a better angle. She closes her eyes and grabs my upper arm. "Oh shit. Oh shit."

I'm not close enough to her, so I pick her up and place her back against the closest wall. Now I can really hold her. I take control of her lips as I continue to thrust into her. I know she's found her release when I feel her walls flutter around me and she screams.

The look of pleasure on her face sends me over the edge. I curse under my breath and press my forehead against hers. I feel like my heart is going to come out of my chest because it's beating so hard. We don't say a word as we cling to each other and catch our breath.

After a few moments Rosa leans her head back against the wall and looks over my shoulder. "We can never eat on that island again."

I laugh and start walking to the bathroom with her still in my arms. Right where she belongs. "We can clean it. Don't worry."

I set her down and we walk into the bathroom. I get a washcloth and two towels from under the sink and set them on the counter. "Get cleaned up. I'll join you when I hear the shower turn on." I kiss her forehead and make my way to the guest bathroom to clean up.

As I'm cleaning up, I realize I haven't thought about work all day. I haven't felt the need to check in with my employees, or randomly stop by to get work done on my day off. I don't think that has ever happened. What the hell is happening to me?

My father is always giving me a hard time about taking some time off every now and then, and not just to go out sailing. I used to love going on hikes and hanging out with Juli and Luca. I couldn't tell you the last time I actually hung out with someone for something other than work. Well, until today. And what an amazing day it has been!

I wash my hands and look up at myself in the mirror. Do I even know who I am anymore? Do I really even know what I want? I've not asked myself in so long. I really don't know anymore.

I hear the shower turn on in my bathroom. I run a hand through my hair. I'm not missing a chance to shower with the most amazing woman I've ever known. No way. This may be the only chance we get. That thought causes my stomach to bottom out and a weird feeling to take over my chest.

I suddenly feel sick. I can't believe I'm going to have to say goodbye to this amazing woman.

I walk in the bathroom and stop in my tracks when I see her. She looks over her shoulder at me, reaches her hand out to me and smiles. "Want to join me?" I take her hand and step in the shower so I can take her in my arms.

All my worries melt away under the stream of warm water and in the embrace of Rosa. My Rosa. My rose. Mine.

24

PRAISED

Rosalie

I CAN'T REMEMBER THE last time someone else washed my hair for me. Even though this situation is strange, this all feels so natural. As natural as breathing.

Matteo leans my head back to rinse my hair. The warm water soothing away my loneliness, my pain. I've not let anyone in since my father died. I couldn't bear the thought of losing someone like that again.

Letting someone in like this gives them the ability to destroy me. To break me. It's a scary thought.

The smell of leather and sandalwood surrounds us. This all feels surreal. Like I'm having an out of body experience. This can't be my life.

A small town girl from Illinois doesn't get to come to Italy and find something like this. I don't even know how to describe what this is between Matteo and I, but I know it's special. This connection. How can either of us develop feelings like this in such a short amount of time? It doesn't make sense.

Matteo runs his hands down my back. I look up at him and watch a water droplet run down his cheek. I reach up and trace its path from his cheek down to his chest. I trace every ridge. I kiss every little freckle formed from spending time in the sun. I can see him so clearly now.

I pour soap on my hands so I can wash him. I start on his chest and move my way around to his back. He deserves to be cherished. Praised.

His eyes are closed when I come back around to his front. I gently place my hand on his cheek. "Look at me."

His eyes spring open. He crowds me against the shower wall and pushes both hands in my hair at the nape of my neck. "I haven't stopped, Rosa."

He kisses me like every woman deserves to be kissed, with confidence and adoration.

Matteo puts the car in park and cuts the engine. It's well after ten o'clock now. The street is unusually quiet and empty.

He grabs my hand and walks with me to the front door of Alda's, then turns to stand in front of me. He settles both hands on the sides of my neck and then uses his thumb to tilt my chin up so I meet his eyes.

"I'll pick you up at eleven in the morning. Make sure you bring your bathing suit." He bends down so he can kiss me on the lips and then my forehead before he opens the front door for me. "Goodnight, Rosa."

I walk backwards into the lobby, unable to look away. "Goodnight."

I close the door behind me and start walking up the stairs to my room. I'm in such a daze I don't even remember unlocking my door. I lay back in the middle of my bed and look up at the ceiling fan. My still damp hair spread out around me. I take in a deep breath and close my eyes.

I lay there for a few minutes, thinking about the day. What an amazing day! I really had such a great time at the market, lunch, making gelato, dinner, what came after dinner—well, everything really. I suddenly remember the photos I took at the market this morning.

I jump up so fast I get a little dizzy and almost fall back down. I grab my laptop and start uploading my photos from the day. I should be writing the article for Foodie, but all I want to do is write a blog post and edit some of my photos from the market.

While my photos are uploading I decide to check all the notifications I ignored on my phone today. I received an email from Susan this morning. Dread fills me as I click on the email. No one wants to hear from Susan in the middle of a job. I've heard horror stories from some of the staff writers. She likes to change things up in the middle of an assignment.

Hello Rosalie,

I hope you're staying on track with your article while on your trip. Let me know if you need anyone to help you. I know the first assignment can be tricky. I just got an email from an old friend in the Potenza area. He just opened a restaurant downtown and wants you to come by next week. I want to make sure his restaurant is featured in the article. I'll attach his address and phone number so you can connect with him. Make sure you feature him toward the beginning of the article. I want him to have a prime spot.

Thanks,
Susan Williams | Editor and Chief, Foodie Magazine

I look at the attachment and do a quick search of the restaurant. I scroll through the search results. A stereotypical tourist joint. Great. I mean, their menu is only pictures. How am I even supposed to be able to tell what I'm eating?

I lay back on the bed again and take another deep breath. I follow the pattern of the texture on the ceiling and contemplate my life choices.

I finally get this big opportunity, and Susan has to hijack the entire thing. I guess it really doesn't matter. I feel like I'm a robot writing that article anyway. I know what's expected of me. Embellish the truth if necessary, sales are key. Feature spots that are most likely to get views and become a trending destination. The same old song and dance, except now, I'm the one that has to do all the writing. It's always been different when I was the one editing. Now I feel like a fake, like I'm not authentic.

I hear my computer ding signaling the upload is complete. I sit up and pull my laptop onto my lap. As I scroll through my photos from today I get butterflies in my stomach. They're so raw and honest. My heart skips a beat when I find one I took of Matteo standing in the kitchen. He had no idea I even took the photo. I had gone to the restroom, and I found him this way when I returned. I couldn't help myself, I had to take a photo. This might be my favorite photo I've ever taken. I won't post that one on my blog though. I couldn't bear to share him with the rest of the world.

I have a feeling most people don't get to see this side of him. In his element. Relaxed. Focused. I'm sure his employees get a glimpse, but not like this. His guard is down. He's vulnerable. It's breathtaking.

I force myself to look away, so I pull up my blog's dashboard in a new tab. 10,000 page views in the last twenty-four hours. Holy shit. Hundreds of messages, comments, and shares. I have to pick my jaw up off the floor. There's no way I'm reading that right. I can't be.

I scroll through my analytics. That's correct. 10,000 people viewed my page. Most of the views came from my last post. I never thought a post titled Street Garden's of the Eden Valley would get so much attention.

I do some digging and find out my blog got shared on a much larger travel site. I've gained over 700 new followers as well. Wow.

I lean back against the headboard and take it all in. I read through all of the comments and reply to as many as I can. Obviously there are some mean comments here and there, but for the most part they are wonderful. It's so fun to hear how much people are enjoying my writing.

A few comments stand out above the rest.

This has inspired me to start my own garden!

I love this! My nana had a garden when I was growing up. She would always let me help tend to it. Some of my best memories. This is a tradition I hope to start with my kids some day.

This made me add the Eden Valley to my travel list!

I can't believe this. I pick up my phone to share the good news. The first person I find myself texting is Matteo.

Me: One of my blog posts went viral!

Matteo: I think you've found your voice, Rosa.

I fire off the same text to Juli and she responds with an animated penguin dance and "Hell yeah!" written at the bottom.

I hit the button to start a new blog post with a smile on my face. I feel like I've found my people, and that's a pretty good feeling.

25

A Thousand Miles

Matteo

I WOKE TO THE smell of her on my sheets. I dreamt of her, of her soft hair draped over my pillow, and of her sweet taste.

I step out of the shower and wrap a towel around my waist. It's almost 10:30. I run my fingers through my wet hair as I walk into my walk-in closet. I've got to hurry if I'm going to stop by the restaurant before I pick her up. I slip a white shirt over my head and pull on my khakis, and grab a pair of swimming trunks, my sunglasses, and a blanket.

I race down the stairs and throw the blanket and my trunks in the back of the car and make my way to Moretti's as quick as I can. I pull into my private parking spot and throw the car in park. I race inside, and my sous chef meets me at the door to hand me what I came here for.

"Cutting it a little close, boss."

I take it from him and look in the basket to make sure everything is in order. I don't want any surprises today.

Everything seems to be in order, so I thank him and head back to my car and place the pickup order with what I already packed. Now it's time to go see my girl.

I pull up at Alda's and jump out of the car. I turn just in time to see Rosa open the door and walk down the steps. I stop and watch her with a smile on my face. She's wearing a white skirt and a tan flowy top today. Her hair is pulled back in a bun with a few pieces around her face. She has a tote bag slung over her shoulder. She's stunning.

She pauses and looks up at me. I swear my heart stops beating when we make eye contact. I take a slow step toward her. I'm sure I have the goofiest smile on my face and I don't give a damn. "Good morning, Rosa."

She smiles right back and starts running toward me. I open my arms and catch her so I can spin her around and kiss her like I've been dreaming about doing since I woke up this morning. I set her back down and she beams up at me. "Good morning, handsome."

"Handsome? I like the sound of that." I kiss her on her nose and take her bag off her shoulder so I can put it in the back of the car. "Ready to go?"

She takes a deep breath and nods her head. "I'm ready."

I open her door for her and she slides in. I jump in the car as well and we get going. "So your blog post went viral?"

She grins over at me. "Yes! I really couldn't believe it when I saw it. My boss did email me last night though. She wants me to include her friend's restaurant in the article. I looked it up and it looks like a tourist trap."

"What's the name of it?"

She scrolls through her phone for a moment. "Here it is. It's called Expedition Italy."

I scrunch up my face. "I know that place. I think the owner's name is Doug or something like that. Their spaghetti sauce comes out of a can. I can't tell you the amount of people who have said they got food poisoning there."

She mimics my facial expression. "Eww."

I nod my head. "Yeah. So what are you going to do about it?"

She sighs and leans her head back against the headrest. "There's nothing I can do. I don't have a choice. I have to include him in the article. If I don't, I'm basically kissing this opportunity goodbye."

"That's shitty."

She thumbs the edge of her skirt. "Yeah. Real shitty. I'll just have to make the best out of it. Maybe he has good desserts or something. Then I could include that and not feel like I'm lying at least."

"That's a shame. I know for a fact he buys his desserts from the frozen section at the supermarket and he barely pays his staff anything."

She throws her hands in the air in defeat. "I guess I'm screwed then."

I rub the stubble on my jaw as I think. I snap my fingers. "I've got it! What if we get Juli to make some dessert pastries and take them over to his restaurant. A lot of local restaurants partner up with bakeries like that. Then you can write about her desserts that are featured there. It'll help her out and get you out of this mess."

She straightens up and turns to face me with a smile on her face. "That's a great idea! I'll call her when we get back later. I know she'd be happy to help. Especially since I'll make sure the name of her cafe is in the article. Susan said I can only write about restaurants and not bakeries or cafes. I've been wondering how to get around that. This is perfect!"

She leans over and kisses me on the cheek. I'm sure I look like a lunatic with how big my smile is. She leans forward and turns the radio volume up. "Oh, I love this song!"

She starts moving her head to the beat, and swinging her arms back and forth. Somehow she has managed to move her head to the beat but not her arms. How does that make any sense? She catches me laughing and she puts her hands up in surrender. "I know. I know. I'm a horrible dancer." She motions toward the lower half of her body. "Even in the car when half my body isn't even involved."

"Don't stop on my account. I am thoroughly enjoying myself."

She gives me a weak punch in the arm and continues dancing. Now she's belting out the lyrics. Very badly I might add. So naturally, I join her when we get to the chorus.

She screams over the music. "You know "A Thousand Miles"?"

I nod my head. "I don't live under a rock! Plus, *White Chicks* is one of my favorite movies." She grins at me as we sing together. She even starts playing fake instruments to the beat. I didn't know one person could bring me this much joy.

An hour later, I turn off the main road and onto a dirt road. I pull the car to the side and shift into park. Rosa sits up straight and takes a look around. "What are we doing? We're not at the coast yet."

I unbuckle my seat belt and turn to face her with a smile on my face. "It's time for lunch." I get out and start gathering my supplies from the back. She scrambles to get out after me.

"Where are we eating? I don't see any buildings around here."

I look at her over the top of the car and hold up the picnic basket I picked up earlier. "I came prepared."

She smiles at me as I walk around to her side of the car. I grab her hand and start pulling her up the dirt road. "Come on. I want to show you something."

We walk up the gentle slope for a few minutes before we get the first glimpse of what we're here to see. She stops dead in her tracks and says so quietly I almost can't hear her. "It's a castle."

She turns to face me with a smile on her face and says much louder this time. "It's a castle! We get to eat lunch in a castle!"

"Well, we get to eat lunch looking at a castle. See that field in front of us?" I point at the field separating us and the castle. She nods her head yes. "It's nothing but mud and unstable ground. That's why no one comes here anymore. The castle is surrounded by it."

She smiles and grabs the blanket that's draped over my shoulder so she can lay it on the ground. "I think it's perfect."

I help her smooth out the blanket and sit down with her. We begin getting our food and drinks out of the basket.

"My grandfather moved to the Amalfi Coast when I was still living in the States. When my dad and I would visit Azzurro in the summer we would always stop for lunch here on our way to visit him. I was obsessed with coming here, so even if it was raining we always had to stop."

She takes a bite of her sandwich and leans back on one elbow so she can look at me. "Why did he move away?"

I look out over the Italian countryside and think back on my childhood. "After my father and I moved away, he decided to follow his dream and move to the coast. He always wanted to be close to the water. My grandmother passed away when I was very young, so he spent most of his adult life raising my father and Alda alone. He deserved to do something for himself."

I can still feel her gaze on me. "Why did you move to Azzurro instead of the Amalfi Coast when you came back?"

I lay back on the blanket and look up into the tree branches above us. "My father always said Azzurro was home, and I'm sure he wanted to be there for Alda and Juli."

I take a bite of my sandwich and wonder what my life would have been like if I moved to the coast after I graduated high school. I wouldn't be as close with Luca. I wouldn't see my father as much. We probably wouldn't own a restaurant together. I never would have met Rosa.

That thought causes a pain in my chest I've never felt before.

I sit up and finish off my sandwich, grabbing water for both of us. Rosa dusts off the crumbs from her hands. "Thank you for bringing me here."

After we each take a drink, we lean back on the blanket and look up at the tree branches and the clouds passing by overhead. She settles her head on my chest and we lay there for a while, tangled up in each other. Right where I want to be.

26

THE WET DREAM

Rosalie

WE PULL INTO THE parking lot of the marina. I'm sad the ride is over to be honest. This has to be the most beautiful place on Earth. The rolling hills turned into mountains that eventually lead to the sea. The coastline is dotted with colorful houses that are perched on the edge of jagged cliffs. It almost doesn't seem real.

My eyes sweep over the crystal blue water. We've had a view of the water for the past twenty minutes or so as we made our way through the town. This would be an artist's paradise. I feel like I'm seeing color for the first time with how vibrant everything is around me.

Seeing the ocean always brings back memories of the last day I spent with my dad. A twinge of pain spreads through my chest as I remember the smile on his face. I smile because even though the pain is still there, I am so thankful for the time we had together.

Matteo reaches over and places his hand on my knee. I look over, but I can barely see him through the tears in my eyes. "He used to sing to me. He would bring his guitar to the beach, and he would sing to me. We would go to the beach often in the evenings when all the tourists were eating dinner. Sometimes we would be the only ones there. I would build sandcastles and look for seashells while he would sit on a towel and sing for me." I catch a tear as it falls down my face. "He kept every shell I ever brought him. Even if they were broken."

A sob suddenly overtakes me. Matteo gathers me in his arms the best he can in the small car. He holds me and lets me cry. After my tears dry up, I wipe off my face and sit up. I look down at his shirt and cringe. "I ruined your shirt."

He doesn't even look down at it. "I can wash it."

I laugh as I wipe my eyes. "The sadness still wins sometimes."

He smiles at me, the acceptance almost doing me in. "It's okay to let the sadness win sometimes."

I straighten up in my seat and pull down the sun visor to look at my reflection in the small mirror. I groan when I see my destroyed eye makeup. "I look like a panda."

Matteo laughs as he opens his car door. "You're a cute panda though."

I playfully smack him on the arm as he gets out of the car. I fix my makeup as best I can before I close the sun visor and open my car door. I take a deep breath as the warm air fills my lungs. The smell of the ocean surrounds me as I gather my bag from the back.

Matteo rounds the back of the car carrying a cooler and a small tote bag. "Just a warning, some of the guys around here can be a little rough around the edges. They're great guys, just used to spending a lot of time on a boat without socializing."

I nod my head as we walk to the dock entrance. "Good to know."

As soon as we step on the dock I hear a deep voice with a thick Italian accent yelling. "Matteo! You fucker! We've not seen you in months."

We stop walking in front of the boat the voice is coming from. It's an old sailboat that has seen better days. The paint is faded and chipping. *The Wet Dream* is written in bold font across the back of the boat. I raise my eyebrows as I look up at Matteo.

I follow Matteo's gaze up the main pole holding the sail until I find a very tan man with snow white hair at the top. He is hanging there without a care in the world. My heart rate picks up just thinking about hanging there without any safety equipment.

Matteo shouts up at him. "Hey Jack! Good to see you. Been a while."

Jack yells back down at us. "Fucking right it's been a while. We don't see you for months, then you show up with a pretty little thing on your arm like that?"

Matteo smiles down at me. "This is Rosalie."

I give a shy wave. I feel very out of place.

Jack gives me a nod and a grin. "Come stay for a while, Matteo! Let's catch up."

Matteo shakes his head and lifts the cooler toward Jack. "We can't. We've got an entire day planned. Maybe next time." He starts walking off without waiting for a reply.

I quickly follow after him. We walk a few more minutes before we stop once more, this time because I think we have arrived at Matteo's boat. This boat is in much better condition compared to Jacks. You can tell this boat has been well looked after. It's mostly white with a blue stripe just above the water line. I reach my hand out to lightly trace the blue letters on the back of the boat. "Bella Sofia?"

"Sofia was my grandmother's name. My beautiful Sofia is what my grandfather would always call her." He reaches out to trace the letters with me. "That was his one condition in his will. I couldn't change the name of the boat. I wouldn't have anyway."

I look up at him and smile. "I wish I could have met them."

He smiles back at me. "Me too." He sets the cooler down and reaches over to unlatch the small gate to the entrance at the back of the boat. "Watch your footing." He holds his hand out to help me safely onto the boat.

After both feet are planted firmly on the ground I take a look around. I can hear Matteo behind me moving the cooler around, but my focus is elsewhere. The part of the boat where the captain would normally sit is covered. It seems to have been an addition to the boat instead of something that was original. I'm very thankful for the shade in either case. I feel like I got a sunburn just from walking to the boat.

There is built-in seating around the front of the boat. I can see two seats that appear to be slightly more worn than the others. That brings a smile to my face imagining Matteo sitting with his grandfather so many years ago.

The edge of the boat is lined with wooden railing. The deck flooring is a rich brown color that is in incredible condition. I turn to find Matteo leaning back against the railing with his arms crossed. "You said you haven't been here in months. How is the boat so clean?"

"I have a deal with the marina to clean the boat once a week. I recommend all my customers use this marina when they want to rent a boat. The marina takes care of my boat in return."

I nod my head as I continue looking around. There are ropes everywhere. I try to follow one to see where it leads with no luck. "This looks complicated."

He walks over to me. "It looks complicated, but this boat is actually set up to be sailed by one person. I can control almost everything from the cockpit."

"A cockpit? Like a plane?"

He laughs as he walks to the enclosed area in the middle. "Kind of. Want to see?"

Excitement takes over as I nod my head. I follow him into the cockpit to find an old fashioned steering wheel surrounded by screens.

Matteo motions for me to sit in the captain's chair and begins pointing at each screen. "I had all these put in a few years ago. This one shows me a video of the anchor while it's being raised or lowered. This one is a map that tracks all nearby boats and the depth of the water. It also allows me to plot my course."

"That's really cool!"

"I'll show you around the cabin and we can take her for a spin!"

I can't keep the smile off my face. This is so much cooler than I expected. I don't know what I was expecting to be honest. An older ship like Jack's that was in horrible condition? I have no idea.

Matteo takes me below deck where the sleeping quarters are and a small restroom. He goes back up to prepare for our trip while I change into my swimsuit.

When I return to the top deck I find him sitting in the captain's seat. His hair is wild from being tossed about by the wind. He seems just as natural in the captain's seat as he does in the kitchen.

I come up behind him and run my hand down his back, his soft shirt gliding under my hand. He leans his head back and smiles at me. His sunglasses are hanging from the collar of his shirt. "Everything is ready to go."

He moves over in the seat to give me room to sit next to him. "Let's do this!"

The way he maneuvers the boat through the marina is amazing. It's a busy day with boats darting here and there, so we move slowly as we exit the marina. As soon as we exit the marina I feel more at ease. Thankful to be out of the crowded docks.

As soon as we start picking up speed, I exit the main cabin to go to the front of the boat. The wind is causing my hair to whip around the back of my head. The salty water splashes up to lightly mist my face. I close my eyes and let myself be in the moment.

27

IT DOESN'T HURT ANY LESS

Matteo

ALONE TIME IS IMPORTANT. It's one of my most valued things.

I never thought I could enjoy my alone time more with another person. Sailing is normally my time. That's why I worked so hard on improving this boat so I could sail alone. Now though—the thought of sailing alone terrifies me. The thought of her not being here is worse.

I watch her through the windows of the cockpit. Her hair is whipping around her. She has her arms stretched out, her palms facing the sky. She's beautiful like this. So carefree.

Bringing her here was different than I expected. I didn't expect to feel so sad. I used to come here every weekend. I don't know how I let myself get so caught up in work that I let myself forget how important this place is to me.

I take a moment to look out at my grandfather's legacy. She's not a fancy yacht like you see so much of on the

Amalfi Coast. She's a classic sailboat, having been built in the 1950's. I'll forever be grateful my grandfather entrusted her to me.

I can't help but wonder what would my grandfather think about me now? Would he be proud of all I have accomplished or would he be disappointed in how much life I have given up living because of work?

I begin lowering the sails as we reach our destination. Rosa lowers her arms and turns to watch the sails descend. I lower the anchor and join her on the deck. "Want to go for a swim?"

I picked this spot because I knew we would be alone. The tourist's boats don't come this way. The water is still crystal clear though. She nods her head and starts walking to the front of the boat to jump off.

I grab her arm as she passes. "You never asked me what was on my bucket list, Rosa."

She raises her eyebrows. "What's on your bucket list?"

A smile encompasses my face. "Skinny dipping."

She shakes her head. "Won't someone see us?"

I shake my head right back. "No one comes out here this time of year."

Her apprehension morphs into a smile. After a few moments she nods her head. "Okay. Let's do it."

I smile as I race to take my clothes off. We toss our clothes toward the cockpit and turn toward the water.

I hold my hand out to her with a smile still on my face. "Together?"

She takes my hand and squeezes it. Her smile lights up her eyes. "Together."

Rosa holds her nose as we jump into the water together. The warm water surrounds us, the bubbles from our entry tickling my sides. My hand still firmly grasping hers, we resurface.

She's laughing so hard she can barely keep herself up. "Now you can check skinny dipping off your bucket list!"

Rosalie

It's 7:30 when we pull up at Alda's. I can barely hold my head up. I'm exhausted and I feel like I've been run over by a bus. I can't wait to go take a shower and get in bed. Matteo gets out of the car and comes around to my side before I can even get my seat belt off. I feel like I'm moving in slow motion. Exhaustion winning the battle. He opens my door, chuckling as he helps me out. "Come on, sleepy head."

"Hey! I'm going as fast as I can mister speedy pants!"

Leaning down, he whispers in my ear. "You didn't call me speedy pants last night. I took my time with you."

My face is bright red as he picks me up bridal style and starts walking to the door. I don't put up a fight because I really don't have the desire to walk up the stairs. When we walk in the front door, Juli is setting the table for dinner.

Juli looks up, and her smile shifts to concern. "Is she alright?"

I open my mouth to answer, but Matteo beats me to it. "She's fine, just tired. We're going to go up and get her stuff."

I lift my head up off his shoulder. "Get my stuff?"

"You're coming home with me." He sets me down at the dining table before pulling a chair out for me. "Stay here and I'll pack your stuff."

I stand there and glare at him with my arms crossed. "Do I have a say in the matter?"

He gives me a smile as he walks up the stairs. "Not really."

I start to walk after him. "Well, what if I don't want to go?"

He stops a few stairs up and turns to face me. "You don't want to go?"

I sigh. "Of course I do. It just would have been nice to be asked."

He steps down one stair. "Fine. Would you like to move in with me for the duration of your stay?"

I walk step past him so I can go to my room. I suddenly don't feel as tired. "Yes. I would like to move in with you for the duration of my stay."

He comes up behind me and scoops me up and throws me over his shoulder. He gives me a little tap on the butt for good measure. "Good."

I look over at Juli as Matteo carries me up the stairs. She smiles up at me. "When you're done you can eat some dinner," she calls, giving me a thumbs up before we disappear around the corner.

When we reach my room, Matteo sets me down in front of my door. I reach into my bag and look for my key. Before I can find it, he spins me around and pushes me back against the wall.

He starts talking so quickly I almost can't keep up. "Are you sure you want to go? I wasn't thinking. I just assumed. I should have asked. I should have—"

I put my hand over his mouth to silence him. "Yes I want to go. Just ask next time."

I can see the relief on his face. I move my hand off his mouth so he can speak. He hangs his head. "I'm sorry. I've never done this before."

I lift his chin up. I can't stand that look on his face. "Done what?"

"This." He motions between us. "A relationship. I don't know what I'm doing. All I know is I can't stand the thought of not spending as much time with you as possible while you're here, and the easiest way to do that is for you to come home with me."

I smile up at him. "I don't know what I'm doing either." I've had relationships here and there, but nothing like this. This is uncharted territory.

"Let's figure it out together then." He kisses me on the lips and steps back so I'll have enough room to open the door. "Let's get your stuff."

I finally find my key and open the door. We quickly pack and go down for dinner. I can hear Alda in the kitchen banging around. Juli walks over, grabbing my arm and pulls me into the reception area.

Matteo shakes his head and laughs. "I guess I'll just go help Alda in the kitchen."

Juli whispers, "What the hell made him act like that?"

I cover my mouth with my hand to try and contain my laugh. "Probably the skinny dipping."

She gasps and grins. "You naughty girl!"

Alda and Matteo are laughing as they walk into the dinning room carrying dishes. Alda sets the dishes down on the table and puts her hands on her hips. "Come on girls, we don't have all night."

Before I know it, dinner is over and we are walking out the front door. It was bittersweet to be honest. The dinner felt like the end of a chapter. Luckily all the other bed and breakfast guests were out tonight, so we got to enjoy dinner with just the four of us.

It feels strange to be leaving, but I can't wait to wake up with Matteo for the rest of my time here in Italy. Matteo is carrying my rolling suitcase and pillow. I've got my camera bag and my purse. I hear the front door open just as we get done loading the car.

Alda comes over and gives me a warm hug. "You're always welcome here."

Why do I feel so emotional? I'm only going down the road. "Thank you for everything."

Juli comes up next and gives me a hug. "This doesn't mean you can't come by and see us. I still expect our lunches everyday."

I laugh as we pull away from the hug. "You can count on it."

Matteo opens the car door for me and I slide in. This is not how I expected this day to end. Not at all. I can't say I mind though. Not one bit.

28

My Beautiful Rose

Matteo

I THOUGHT I FUCKED it all up. I thought I had ruined everything. And I have to say, that didn't sit well with me. Not one bit. We walk into my condo and my heart is still in my throat. I need to do better. Be better. For her.

I drop her bags in the living room and pick her up so I can throw her over my shoulder. She giggles as I walk down the hallway. "Where are you taking me?"

"To bed."

"But we need a shower."

"Fine. I'll fuck you in the shower then." I flip on the lights and turn on the water. I set her down on the counter and step back to look at her. She's breathing heavily. Her hair still smells like saltwater. Her face is bare. She's perfect. And she's mine.

I pull my shirt over my head and toss it to the ground. I walk over to her slowly. Her breathing grows heavier with every step I take. "I'm going to worship you now, Rosa."

I lightly trace a line down her arm with my finger. "Every inch of your beautiful body." I tilt her head back to give me access to her neck. "My beautiful rose."

I kiss down her neck to her collarbone. My pants are stretched to their limit. I groan when she runs her fingernails down my back. I quickly reach up and pull her shirt over head and throw it across the room. I can't wait any longer. I untie the back of her bikini top and let it fall to the floor. With a feather light touch I run my finger over her nipple. She takes in a shuddered breath and tilts her head back. I kiss her softly as I undo the button on her shorts. I unzip them and let them fall so they pool around her ankles. I untie the sides of her bikini bottoms and step back to look at her. She steps out of both and kicks them to the side. Perfection.

I hook my thumbs in my trunks and push them down my legs. I step out of them and her eyes trace my naked body. I palm my cock and the fire in her eyes intensifies.

I walk to her slowly, not wanting to rush this moment. When I reach her, our mouths collide. She runs her fingers through my hair. I pick her up and she latches her legs around my waist. My cock is pressed against her entrance, begging for release. I reach into the shower to turn on the water, waiting for it to be warm before I walk us under the stream of water.

I push her against the tile and reach between us to find her dripping wet for me. She moans as I push a finger inside her. I find her clit with my thumb and she bows her back off the tile. I continue to rub my thumb on her clit as I push another finger into her. She digs her nails into my back and tightens her legs around my waist as she finds her release.

I pull my hand away and position myself at her entrance. I don't give her time to come down from the high before I push into her with one thrust. We both moan as I bottom out inside her. I don't move. Our foreheads meet and we close our eyes. Taking it all in. She was made for me.

I press a kiss to her mouth. I kiss her like she's the oxygen I need to survive. I start to move and I almost lose it. It takes everything in me to hold myself back. I reach one hand up and stroke her clit as I pick up my pace. She breaks our kiss and leans her head back against the wall.

"Oh shit!"

I can feel her tightening around me. "That's it, Rosa. Come for me."

Her release sends me over the edge. I cry out her name as I spill my release inside her. Neither of us move as we try to catch our breath. The warm water is still running over us. I don't know how sex with Rosa just keeps getting better. That doesn't seem possible. When we finally catch our breath, I pull out and set her on her feet.

She sways and leans back against the wall. I wrap an arm around her waist so she doesn't fall. "I guess my legs forgot how to work."

A laugh escapes me as I kiss her forehead. "You're welcome."

She gives me a weak push and laughs. "Cocky much?"

I shift our bodies so I can wash her hair. "Only all the time."

She moans as I begin massaging shampoo into her scalp. "You're spoiling me."

"You deserve it."

We take our time washing each other. Spoiling each other. When we're done, we step out and dry off. Rosa wraps the towel around her hair. "I'll need to get my hair brush and stuff."

I wrap the towel around my waist and open the bathroom door. "I'll go get your bags, but don't you dare put clothes on."

She giggles as I walk down the hallway to gather her bags. I smile to myself as I think about how good it feels to have her here. It feels like all is right in the world.

I collect all of her bags and her pillow, and carry them to my room. I don't know why she's kept this raggedy pillow.

I set her bags down at the foot of the bed and then start towards the bathroom. Rosa is drying her hair, without a stitch of clothes on. I lean against the doorway, cross my arms over my chest, and take her in. She's still flushed from our shower. "I could get used to this."

She looks over her shoulder and smiles at me. "Get used to what?"

"You, being here. Naked."

She throws the towel at me and I catch it before it can hit my face. "You just want me naked."

I throw the towel back at her and it hits her square in the middle of her face. "I just want you here." I shrug. "It would just be nice if you were naked."

She smiles and shakes her head. She pauses to look around the room. When she can't find what she's looking for she holds up the towel. "Laundry hamper?"

I point to the closet door. "In there."

She opens the door to the closet and flips on the light. Her eyes go wide and she spins on her toes to look at me. "You forgot to show me your closet when you gave me the tour. This is huge!"

I rub the back of my neck and step up behind her to look around at the mostly empty space. I have a lot of clothes, but not nearly enough to fill the space. "You're more than welcome to unpack and hang up your clothes in here. I've got plenty of extra hangers."

She gets a big smile on her face. "That would be great! I didn't have much hanging space at Alda's. My dresses have been getting wrinkled."

I've never even brought a girl back to my place, let alone given them full rein of my closet. What the hell happened to me? Rosa. That's what's happened to me.

She opens her bag and begins unpacking. "I'll unpack the rest of my clothes tomorrow. I just need my toiletries tonight."

She walks back out into the steamy bathroom to begin unpacking her toiletry bag. I lean against the closet doorway and watch as she makes her mark on my bathroom. She slowly unpacks all her toiletries and lays them out on my bathroom vanity. I walk over and open an empty drawer, "You can use this."

"Are you sure? I feel like I'm taking over."

"I've never been more sure of anything."

She stops unpacking and looks over at me. "I'm scared, Matteo. I'm scared of how much you mean to me."

I go over and scoop her up and sit her on the one empty spot left on the counter. I push her wet hair out of her face and step between her legs. "I know the feeling, Rosa. I know the feeling." I run my hand down her spine and I feel her shiver. I take a small step back. Just enough so I can look down at her beautiful face. "Come to bed with me, Rosa."

She traces a line down my chest to my belly button without taking her eyes off mine. "Are we going to be sleeping?"

"Eventually."

Rosalie

I slowly open my eyes. For a moment I forget where I am. That is, until I feel a warm body pressed up behind me and a strong arm draped over my waist. I smile as I think about our first night together. I rub my thighs together and feel the slight sting that confirms it wasn't a dream.

"Good morning, Rosa." He tightens his grip around me and pulls me back even tighter against his bare chest. I wiggle my butt back against his already very firm rod that is poking me in the ass.

"Good morning. Did you sleep well?"

He laughs as he buries his face in my neck. "What little sleep I had was wonderful."

"Now whose fault was that?"

He reaches down and pinches my butt under the covers. "Definitely yours."

I try my hardest to act offended. "Hey! It takes two to tango, buddy!"

He flips me on my back and settles between my legs. He tickles me along my rib cage and I start to squirm. "Buddy? I think I'm a little more than a buddy. Don't you, Rosa?" I try to speak, but the only noise that I can make is a squeak followed by deep belly laughs. "What was that? I'm sorry I can't understand you. Would you mind speaking up a bit?" I try my best to wiggle free, but I fail miserably. "Come on, Rosa. I taught you better than that. How are you supposed to get out of a hold like this?"

It's hard to think in a situation like this, but I get my wits about me and raise my knee up so I can hit him in his most sensitive area. Before I have a chance he picks up on my move and finally stops his tickle torture. He moves off me and lays on his side to allow me to catch my breath. My sides are burning from the laughter. "Good girl."

I'm still huffing and puffing trying to catch my breath, so I'm sure I sound like an injured animal. "That wasn't fair. That was totally not a realistic situation."

He props himself up on one arm. "No, it wasn't. The real thing would be much worse. It was still good practice though."

I guess I can't argue with that.

29

EXPEDITION ITALY

Rosalie

I shake the water off my umbrella before walking into Juli's cafe for a late lunch. She pops her head up from behind the counter and sighs with relief when she sees me. "It's just you. Thank fuck."

I put my elbows on the counter and lean over to see what she's working on. She's bent down behind the counter with tools spread all over the floor. "Bad day?"

She pushes the hair out of her face with the back of her hand and grabs the edge of the counter for support while she stands. "You have no idea."

She grabs our sandwiches and some chips before we sit at a table in the corner. I grab a handful of chips and stuff them in my mouth. "Want to talk about it?"

She slumps back in her seat and hangs her head. I've never seen her like this. Normally she's the one cheering me up. Not the other way around. "It has been a day from hell. It was raining when I woke up this morning. I hate the rain. Then, my coffee machine broke, so no coffee for me. And that disaster of a machine decided to poop soaked coffee grounds all over me before I left the house."

She raises her hands up in the air and motions to the ceiling. "I should have taken all that as a sign from the heavens not to leave my house this morning. See this shirt?" She pulls on the edges of her stained shirt for emphasis. "This is my third shirt of the day." I open my mouth to ask what else happened, but she holds her hand up to silence me. "Don't ask."

I sit back in my seat and accept my fate. "How did it go taking the pastries to Expedition Italy? Thanks for that by the way."

She gets up and starts pacing the room. "I was getting there. Before I can even walk into that horrid restaurant a car drives by when I'm walking on the sidewalk and splashes muddy water all over me." She motions in a circle around her head. "Thankfully he missed my hair, but he ruined one of my favorite pairs of jeans."

I take my first bite of my sandwich and watch as she paces a hole in the floor.

"Then, when I finally get there, this guy opened the front door and smacked me right in the face. That causes me to drop one of the boxes of pastries all over the ground.

Well, I don't think guy is the right word, more like a scary badass." I open my mouth again, and she holds her hand up to prevent me from saying anything. "Don't worry, there were a few other boxes, it just pissed me off. Then I finally make it back here and my oven is broken. Again. That's why I have this shit all over my shirt."

She finally sits back down. She lets out a long breath and rubs her temples. "Please tell me something good has happened to you today." She sits up straighter. "Oh I know! Tell me about your first few days living with Matteo." She scrunches her nose. "Leave out anything sex related, I don't need that vision in my head."

I laugh at her while I keep eating my lunch. "You're a mess."

She takes a chip from my plate and pops it in her mouth. "But I'm your mess." She wipes her hands on her pants before she sits back in her chair. "Tell me about your marketing ideas for Moretti's. If all goes well I may have to get you to help me out around here."

I wipe my hands on a napkin and shake my head. "Talk to me again after I get done over there today. I'm kind of freaking out about it to be honest. I feel like I'm way out of my depth here."

She smacks her hand on the table and points at me.

"You are Rosalie freaking Auclair! Get your head out of your ass for two seconds so you can see how amazing you are! I mean, come on! Have you seen your blog? Girl, you are killing it! Don't you dare try to argue with me."

"But—"

"No buts! Do I need to go tell Matteo you are over here talking shit about yourself or do I need to whip your ass myself?"

I smile and shake my head. "You sound so American sometimes. No. He would freak out and give me a lecture about how awesome I am or something."

"As he should! And don't ever say I sound like an American again."

I take the last bite of my sandwich and put my napkin on my plate. "You're a really good friend, you know that right?"

"You're a really good friend, you know that right?"

She finishes off the last of her sandwich and starts stacking our plates. "Duh. Now let's go pick out some dessert. I'll put yours in a bag so you can take it with you. Make sure you get something for Matteo too." Everyone needs a friend like Juli. She hands me a bag with all my goodies. "Let me know how it goes with the marketing stuff and with Expedition Italy tonight. I'll see you this weekend at

Luca's party. This is my last weekend before I have Gemma for a few weeks."

I nod my head as I start walking to the door just as another customer comes in. I forgot she was taking care of her niece while her sister and her husband are out of town. I thank Juli for lunch and battle with my umbrella for far too long before I finally make it out the door into the pouring rain. I stand on the curb for a moment and take in the beauty of the Eden Valley.

A car drives by and I close my eyes so I can listen to the sound the tires make as they go through the water on the road. I can hear a bell ring as a shop door opens and closes a few doors down. I can smell the fresh baked bread from the bakery down the street. I can hear the rain drops hitting my umbrella.

"Hello, Rosa."

I open my eyes and see Matteo walking across the street with a smile on his face. He parked his car in front of Alda's place. A huge smile takes over my face. "Hello, handsome."

He comes up on the sidewalk and sweeps me up in his arms. I drop my umbrella and wrap my arms around his neck. He sets me down and picks my umbrella up off the ground so he can keep the rain off us. "I missed you." He pulls me in close. Right where I want to be. The smell of sandalwood and leather wrapping me in a warm blanket.

"I was only gone for a few hours."

He puts his hand on his heart. "Are you saying you didn't miss me?"

I lightly push him on the shoulder. "Of course I did."

He kisses me on the nose. "That's what I thought. Ready to go?"

We cross the street toward his car. "As ready as I'll ever be."

30

SEEING IS BELIEVING

Rosalie

MY PALMS ARE SWEATY and I feel like I'm going to faint.

All eyes are on me as I set up all my camera gear and lights. Why couldn't we have done this while the restaurant is closed? All I need is for everyone to watch me fumble around with my setup.

I know. I know. I want fresh food and some of the employees in my shots. I just need to deal with it. I've just never been the one in charge of something like this. I take a deep breath to center myself. I can do this. If I have a freakout moment it's not going to make this any easier.

I shake out my arms to try and bring the circulation back to them. I wonder if that's normal? Probably not.

Okay. I'm ready.

One of the cooks brings over my first dish and I begin the staging process. Matteo brought me a mountain of props earlier, so this should actually be fun. I start arranging the scene and it's like everything around me fades away. The sound of all the clattering of dishes and the sizzling of food cooking on the stove melts into the background. I can no longer smell the freshly cooked pasta sauce on the table next to me. It's just me and the camera.

Before I know it, I've taken over a hundred photos and I have pages and pages of notes for social media marketing ideas. I can't wait to use some of these photos on my blog later. I pull my phone out of my pocket and look at the time. I've been at this for a few hours. I should probably take a break. Plus, I just realized I've really got to pee.

I look around but don't see Matteo anywhere. His office door is closed. I'm sure he's busy. I'll just go use the restroom and get back to work. Before I go to the restroom, I start uploading my photos to my laptop. I don't want to lose all the photos I've worked so hard for. Better to be safe than sorry. I put my lens cap back on and store my camera away in my bag. I reach my arms up to stretch my back and crack my neck.

I make my way to the staff bathroom by the sinks where all the dishes are washed. When I'm done I splash some water on my face and rub the back of my neck with a cold towel. It can get so hot in the kitchen with all the stoves and ovens going all the time. I dry off my face and open the door to go back out into the kitchen.

I'm surprised to find Lorenzo standing next to my table. He smiles when he sees me coming. "Hello Rosalie. It's so nice to finally meet you. Mind if I sit?" He motions to a chair next to the table I've taken over with all my camera gear.

"No, not at all. Go right ahead. It's so nice to finally meet you as well." I sit and turn to face him so I can devote all my attention to the man that raised the most amazing man I know.

He points at all my camera gear. "This is quite the setup you have here. Can I see some of your photographs?"

I open my laptop so I can pull up some of the photos I just took. "Sure! They're not edited yet, but you'll be able to get an idea of how they will turn out."

He pulls his glasses out of his shirt pocket and puts them on. I show him how to flip through the photos with the arrow keys. He takes a few minutes to look through all the photos. I tell him about the plans we have for each shot. I want his opinion about all this stuff, so I hold my breath while I await his reaction. When he is done, he sits back in his seat and takes his glasses off and stores them away. "Those are amazing, Rosalie. You have a real gift."

I can't keep the smile from taking over my face. "I'm glad you like them. I have so many fun ideas on how to bring in business."

He crosses one leg over the other and puts his hands in his lap. "Tell me about your ideas."

I proceed to tell him about all the ideas Matteo and I have been talking about over the past few days. I mention creating a website and social media accounts. He sits quietly while I talk. When I get done, he nods his head and scratches his chin. "I see. And you think this will actually bring in that many new customers without losing our originality?"

I nod my head, hopeful he will see how important this could be to his business. "I do."

He sits up straighter in his seat. "I think you have some great ideas. We're lucky to have you here to help us. I'm useless when it comes to things like this."

I smile as I look him in the eye. I want to see his reaction. "Actually, most of them are Matteo's ideas. I'm just making them a reality."

Shock takes over his face. "What? He's never shown me anything like this before."

I shake my head. "He just didn't have a way to show you what he meant until now. That's what I'm helping him with."

He rubs his hand over his face just like his son. "I had no idea."

I close my laptop lid. "It's okay. Sometimes we just need to be shown before we can believe in something."

When he smiles at me like this, it's like Matteo is staring back at me. "He's lucky to have you."

I smile back at him. "We're lucky to have each other."

His smile shifts to a softer one. "You're very good for my son. Since you arrived, Matteo has actually been living. I've not seen him this happy in years. I have always tried to push him to take more time off and actually enjoy life. It seems like he's finally found his reason. He will be devastated when you leave."

I look down at my lap and beg the tears to stay away. "I will be devastated when I leave."

He reaches out and gently places his hand on my shoulder. I look up into his kind eyes. "Do you want to leave?"

I fidget in my seat. "No, but the thought of not going back terrifies me."

"Making big changes can be scary. At the end of the day you have to do what's best for you."

I tuck a stray hair behind my ear. "That's the thing, I always thought writing was what was best for me. My dad always told me how good I was at it, so I thought that was the best direction for me to go in. Now I'm not sure what to do. I seem to have lost my passion for it."

Lorenzo shakes his head and smiles. "Matteo has shown me your blog. That is not the work of someone who has lost their passion. I think your passions have shifted." The bell suddenly dings signaling there is an order ready. He turns to look across the kitchen. "I better get that. We're quite busy today."

We both stand and he pulls me into a hug that takes my breath away. Hugging him feels just like hugging my father. I feel tears gather in my eyes. I wish so badly he could have met Matteo. We pull apart from the hug and he gives me a big smile before he walks away. I get a tissue out of my bag and dab the corners of my eyes. I still have a smile on my face when I get back to work.

31

SUBMIT

Rosalie

MATTEO STOPS NEXT TO the curb in front of Juli's cafe. He puts the car in park and takes his sunglasses off. "Are you sure you don't want to come?"

I put my elbow on the center armrest and lean over and kiss him. "I'm sure. I've never rock climbed a day in my life. I would just hold you guys back. You deserve a guys day. Plus, I'm excited to spend the day with Juli."

Movement catches my eye. I look up to find Luca walking out of Juli's holding a bag full of goodies and two drinks. A grin the size of Texas on his face, his dimple on full display.

I reach back to get my bag. "You'll have a great time at the climbing gym."

He sighs. "I know. I just don't want to waste one of our days together."

I put my bag on my shoulder, and open my door so I can get out of the car. "I know, but if I don't spend some time with Juli, she's going to kill us both."

He grins and leans toward me. "Fine. Have a good time. Text if you need anything."

I lean forward to give him a long kiss.

Luca comes up behind me and laughs. "Get a room, kids."

We separate from the kiss and I fully get out of the car, but not before Matteo can give me a tap on the butt. I give him a smile before I start walking across the street. "Have a good time guys."

Luca sets his gear down and waves. "Bye, Rosa. Don't have too much fun without us today! "

Matteo reaches out and lightly punches him in the stomach. "Ouch!" He rubs his stomach. "I mean Rosalie." His voice becomes muffled as I walk across the street. "Come on man, you can't assault someone for using a nickname."

I shake my head and laugh as I walk through the door. Juli pulls her apron over her head and hangs it on a hook behind the counter. "Finally! I'm so ready for this day!" She starts loading the cash from the register into a small bag she keeps hidden when the cafe is open. "Flip the sign for me!"

I back track to the door and flip the sign to closed. "Are you sure it's okay to close early?"

She nods her head dramatically. "Oh yeah. This week has been hell. We deserve a girls day."

She hands me a coffee cup and a muffin. I groan, "You are the best."

She smiles as she takes the large clip out of her hair, and her long hair falls down her back as she runs her fingers through it. "I know! Now let's go! My nails need some serious attention."

We walk down the street to a local nail salon. I'm not normally one to get my nails done, but Juli insisted we get all dolled up for Luca's party tomorrow night. I go for a light pink polish. Juli picks a bright red that she claims will match her dress for the party perfectly.

After we are done there, we walk next door to a cafe. We pick a seat outside and start looking at the menu. I've learned a handful of words while I've been here, but deciphering a menu isn't something I can do. I hold my menu out to Juli, pointing to an option. "What is this?"

Juli leans forward and looks at the item I'm pointing at. "That's a salad with olives, tomatoes, and a variety of peppers. It says you can add chicken if you want."

I nod my head. "That sounds pretty good."

She hums while she further examines the menu. "That's not like you. You normally go for something that will stand out more in your article."

I put my menu down and lean forward. "About that."

She puts her menu down and grins at me. "Yeah?"

I uncross my legs so I can lean even closer. "The article is done."

She squeals and throws her hands up in the air. "No way! You're free! How did you manage to add in Expedition Italy?"

"Your desserts saved the day. I made sure to give him my compliments about the desserts only. You should be expecting a call soon about becoming one of his vendors."

She rolls her eyes. "Great."

"I never said you had to accept."

She takes a sip of her sparkling water before saying, "That's true. Have you submitted the article to Susan yet?"

I shake my head. "No."

She puts her hands down on the table. "What the hell are you waiting for?"

I shrug. "I guess I don't know what I want the outcome to be."

She tilts her head to the side. "You mean you want to stay?"

I play with a stand of my hair. "I don't know. I do, but what if Matteo doesn't want me to stay? What if I stay and everything changes?"

She picks up a bread stick and points at me with it. "Are you crazy? That man is head over heels for you, girl."

I smile. "So what do I do?"

She sits up straighter in her seat. "Submit the article. Who knows, you might not even get the job. Then the decision will be made for you."

"But what if I do get the job?"

She leans forward and puts her elbows on the table. "Then you decide from there. If you don't submit it, you'll always wonder if you were capable or not."

I nod my head. "You're right. I would always wonder what if."

She moves the items around on the table to clean a space in front of me. "Submit it now."

I lean back in my seat, much more quickly than I intended. "What? I can't do it now."

"You said it was finished, right?"

I nod my head. "Well, yeah."

"Then there's nothing to wait on! If you don't do it now you'll overthink it for the rest of the weekend."

I nod my head. She has a point. I might as well do it and get it over with. I pull out my laptop from my bag and type up the email. I attach my article and one of my blog posts, and hit submit.

Matteo

I pull myself up onto the top of the wall and sit. That boulder kicked my ass. It's been way too long since I've done any kind of rock climbing. Lifting boxes at the restaurant apparently doesn't work the same muscles as rock climbing.

Luca pats my shoulder. "I knew you'd make it eventually." The fucker isn't even out of breath.

I lightly push on his shoulder before I lay back to catch my breath. "That was a V6 you ass."

"All I heard is you're mid level now. You used to be able to do V8's like they were nothing."

I laugh, still out of breath. "Yeah, three years ago when we used to do this every other day."

Most climbing gyms don't have tall enough ceilings for you to be able to sit on top of the walls. This new gym is nice, even if it is over an hour away from home. I wipe the chalk off my hands onto my pants and get my phone out of my pocket so I can check my notifications.

Luca laughs, "You checked your phone fifteen minutes ago. Rosalie is fine, man."

I slide my phone back in my pocket. "I know. I just want to make sure she doesn't need anything."

"What could she possibly need? I'm sure the girls are having a great time."

I lay back to stare at the ceiling. "I know. That doesn't keep me from worrying."

He lays back with me. Our feet slightly dangling off the edge. "She's changed you." I look over at my best friend, the person who knows me better than I know myself, and raise my eyebrows. He puts his hands up. "I'm not saying that's a bad thing."

I look back up at the ceiling and smile.

"She's good for you. I'm happy you found her."

"Me too."

32

ZIPPER

Matteo

MY RESTAURANT IS A madhouse. People are running around everywhere. There's a few people setting up tables around the edges of the room. A few others are hanging decorations along the walls. I'm trying like hell to make sure no one breaks anything.

Luca is going to lose his shit when he sees the fuss everyone is making over his birthday. If it was up to him, it would be a few close friends having dinner or something. His mom insisted we go all out since this is his first year of training. The next year and a half will be very busy.

I turn when I hear Rosa's voice. She must have just walked out of the kitchen. She's already dressed for the party tonight. Her short dark blue dress fits tightly against her beautiful body. Her hair flowing in loose curls down her back.

One of my employees brings a stack of boxes of desserts out of the kitchen and sets them on the table in front of Rosa. She quickly begins emptying the boxes of their contents and placing the various desserts that Juli made on serving trays and displays. I could sit and watch her work all night. Her confidence is shining throughout the room.

I never thought I would enjoy having someone to work with, someone I can depend on like this. We continue moving around the room as a team, filling in where the other can not. I watch as she works her magic on the center pieces. I work through the plan for the evening for the final time with my employees.

I walk back into the kitchen to find Rosa in my dad's office laughing so hard her face is bright red. She's standing in the middle of the small room looking at the wall of photos. I stop for a moment, not wanting to interrupt their conversation. My dad places a photo back on the wall and points at another slightly farther up. "This one was from our fishing trip the summer before he went to high school."

She steps closer to the photo. I can tell she's smiling. "He looks so handsome."

My dad puts his hands in his pockets and laughs. "And stubborn too. He would not stop until he caught this big bass he swore he had seen go under the rock that morning. Turns out that was a record breaking fish in that camp ground." He shakes his head. "I never doubted him for a second. So many other campers told him to give it up. We sat there for over eight hours that day. Everyone begged him to keep the bass, but he let it go."

I feel a smile form on my face as I think back on the memory. The sacrifices my dad made to give me the best childhood did not go unnoticed. We didn't have the nicest vacations, but they were filled with the best memories.

Rosa steps forward and picks up a picture frame that is sitting on dad's desk. "What about this one?"

I know what photo it is just by looking at the frame. My dad sighs and takes the photo from her. He rubs his thumb across the glass to push the dust away. "This one is my favorite. This was the first time I saw him smile after we moved back here. He decided he wanted to make dinner for us after I got home from work. He worked for hours on that ribollita soup." He laughs. "It was the worst soup I've ever had."

I smile. That was the first dish I ever made on my own. I had found an old cookbook in the kitchen. I tried to pick the easiest meal I could to fix us that night.

My dad hands Rosa the photo once more. Rosa runs her fingers along the frame's edge. "His ribollita has improved since then."

My dad just laughs. "It sure has."

My smile only grows. Of course she would remember what we fixed for our first date. She sets the photo back down on my dad's desk. "Thank you for showing me all your photos. They are lovely."

My dad pulls Rosa in for a hug. "Anytime, my dear." He looks over her shoulder to smile at me.

I leave them alone and retreat to my office with a smile on my face. A few moments later I hear a small knock on my door. I turn in my chair to face the door. "Come in."

The door cracks open and Rosa walks in. "Can you help me with something?"

I stand and reach out for her. "Anything." She accepts my hand. I trail my hand up her arm until I reach her neck.

She spins so her back is facing me and gathers her hair to one side, exposing a red patch of skin on the back of her neck. "The hem tag of this dress is killing me. Do you think you can cut it out for me?"

I turn to look at my desk, hoping to find something to help me cut the tag. "I mostly work with digital papers, so I don't have any scissors in here."

She digs in her bag to produce some small nail clippers. She hands them to me over her shoulder. "Will these work?"

I take them from her and inspect them. "Probably. Hold still."

I slowly start unzippinging her dress to reveal more of the red patch. The rest of her beautiful skin is flawless. It takes me a moment to work the tag free of the stitching. I run my thumb over where the tag originated to find a smooth surface.

When I'm finished I run the palm of my hand down the uninjured part of her back. Chill bumps follow in my wake. I follow the curve of her ribs until my palm is resting on her stomach under her dress. She releases a shuddered breath as I work my way up to find her bare breasts. I gently roll one nipple between my index finger and thumb. I feel my cock go rock hard in my suit pants, the zipper cutting into me. I release her breast and move my hand up to slide one of her straps off her shoulder. I run my nose along the side of her neck. She leans her head to the side to give me better access.

She leans forward to lock the door before she spins around in my arms. Her other dress strap falls from the movement, her chest on full display. I lean forward and kiss her slowly. "You'll have to be quiet, Rosa."

She nods her head as I kiss her again, this time more powerful, hungry. I reach between her legs to find her soaked thong. Groaning, I push the fabric to the side and stroke her. I hold her up as her knees buckle. I spin her in my arms and push her down on my desk. I push her thong down her legs and free myself from my pants. My cock throbs in my hand at the sight of her laid out below me.

I run my throbbing head through her wet folds and groan as I slowly enter her. She lays her cheek down on my desk and squirms. A small moan escapes her. I push her hair out of her face and bend down to whisper in her ear. "Be quiet now, Rosa. Those moans are just for me." She reaches up and puts her hand over her mouth as I begin to move. "Good girl."

My rhythm builds as she squeezes me. Music starts in the main room, but I still fight to keep myself quiet. We find our release together. Panting and exhausted, we catch our breath before I pull out of her and grab a tissue from my desk to clean myself up. I pull her to me with one hand and kiss her. When we pull away I run my thumb across her cheek. "I'm glad you're here, Rosa."

She smiles up at me as she pulls her thong back up her legs. "Me too." She kisses me on the cheek and straightens her hair. "I'm going to go clean up."

I watch her walk out of my office with a smile on my face.

33

THE PARTY

Rosalie

I WALK OUT OF the bathroom and head straight for Juli. I tried my best to make it look like Matteo didn't just screw my brains out in his office. Not sure if I succeeded. When I finally make it to Juli's table I'm slightly out of breath.

She sets her drink down and laughs as she leans close to whisper, "Next time you want to fuck in public, make sure you're not banging the desk against the wall. I'm scarred for life."

My face goes pale. "You could hear us?"

She laughs, "I think I was the only one. I turned the music up to drown out the banging. You're lucky everyone has already moved out to the main room from the kitchen."

I put my hand over my mouth and laugh. "Well that's not embarrassing at all."

She shrugs. "It happens to the best of us."

Matteo and Luca arrive at the table at almost the same time. Matteo bends down to kiss me on the forehead. He places a drink in front of me and gives me a wink as he lowers himself into his chair next to me.

I look over at Luca. He's looking around the room with disgust written all over his face. "Happy birthday, Luca."

He turns to me and smiles. "Thanks Rosalie. I can't believe my mom talked me into all this."

I grab my drink and hold it in front of me. "Let's at least make the most of it. Cheers to new friends."

We all clink our drinks together and take a drink. I see Lorenzo walk into the kitchen out of the corner of my eye, followed by a few employees. A moment later big serving plates are being carried out and placed on the buffet table.

Matteo stands and clears his throat. Someone turns the music down, and everyone turns to look in our direction. "Thank you all for coming tonight to celebrate my best friend. You're a blessing to all of us, Luca." He raises his glass. "Cheers to the birthday boy." I hear an echo of cheers around the room. Matteo motions to the buffet table. "Dinner is served."

Luca goes first through the line. We all pile our plates high with way too much food, especially because we hit the dance floor as soon as we get done eating.

Matteo spins me around as we dance in the middle of the dance floor surrounded by our friends. Juli and I take turns singing "You're the One that I Want" from the movie

Grease. Matteo and Luca laugh so hard I'm surprised they don't pass out.

Juli grabs my hand at the end of "Shake It Off" by Taylor Swift, "Let's go out front to cool down." She fans her face with her hand. "It's getting so hot in here." I nod my head and look at Matteo to let him know where we're going.

He must have heard her because he leans down next to my ear and says, "I'll join you later. I've got to check on the kitchen."

I nod my head and follow Juli off the dance floor. We grab out bags from the table and fan our faces as we wait for a few waters at the bar in the back of the room. I think I've had enough alcohol for the night. The cool night air is a relief as we walk out the front door. I pull my hair up off my neck and sit down on the curb. "I hadn't realized it was so hot in there."

Juli sits next to me. She holds her cold glass to her cheek. "I know. I was roasting. It's so fun to see Matteo loosen up a bit. I'm used to seeing Luca have a good time, but Matteo never dances. Ever."

I laugh, "They seem to be having fun. I guess Luca isn't as upset about the party as he was letting on."

Juli shakes her head. "He loves all the attention." She suddenly sits up straight. "Hey! Did you hear back about the job?"

I shrug. "I have no idea. I haven't checked my email."

"Aren't you excited to find out if you got the job?"

I shake my head. "No. Not really. I'm kind of scared to find out to be honest."

She holds out her hand. "Give me your phone and I'll look. Knowing is better than not knowing."

I pull my phone out of my bag, unlock it, and hand it to her. She scrolls through my phone for a few agonizing moments before she settles her finger over the screen. "You got the email."

My heart drops. What do I want the answer to be? Do I even care? I guess I really just want to know if I was capable of getting the job after all this time.

She clicks the screen. I can see her eyes moving back and forth as she reads. Her face lights up as she looks up at me, I barely hear the front door of the restaurant open and close behind us. "You got the job!"

A smile spreads across my face. I did it. After all these years. I look behind us to find Matteo standing there, a hurt look on his face.

I stand to go to him, wanting to share the good news. As soon as I stand the front door opens and an employee runs out, panic consuming his face.

Matteo

"That's fine. Just put out some more sides. No one will notice if we run out of a few things."

The crowd is a bit bigger than expected. I didn't even realize we knew this many people. I make my way through the kitchen to my dad's office. His door is open, but I knock anyway. "Everything okay back here?"

He looks up from his desk. His face is a bit more red than usual. This place is getting hotter by the minute with all the people dancing. Maybe I should open the doors and windows for a while.

He smiles and nods his head. "All good. Go enjoy yourself."

I make my way back out to the main room to grab some water and ask an employee to open the windows and doors before I go out to sit with Rosa and Juli. I spot Luca dancing with a few girls we knew in high school. He has a shit eating grin on his face. I just shake my head and walk out the front door.

The smile fades from my face as soon as I hear four simple words come out of Juli's mouth, "You got the job!" Rosa's face lights up.

I feel like my world just crashed down around me. Like I'm free falling and there's nothing I can do to stop the fall. I shouldn't be surprised. This is what she was here for after all. We haven't talked about this, I guess that's my fault. I just thought we had more time. Rosa spots me. She gets up off the curb to come to me. I already feel myself withdrawing, putting up walls to protect myself.

I'm bracing myself to hear the words I have dreaded since I looked into her eyes in that disgusting shed on the side of the road, covered in mud and soaked to the bone. But before she gets the chance, one of my employees rushes out the door. There is panic written all over his face and I go rigid.

"Matteo! It's your dad! I think he's having a heart attack!"

My heart drops for a second time tonight. This time for an entirely different reason. I'm running before I can even comprehend what is happening. The music is still playing and there are people on the dance floor.

I catch Luca's eye and his face shifts to confusion. He moves through the dance floor and is by my side in seconds. "What's wrong?"

I can barely form a complete sentence. "It's my dad."

I bust through the kitchen doors and I'm met with pandemonium. People running everywhere. I think someone is crying, but I can't be sure. All I can see is the lifeless body of my father laying on the ground. I hear someone on the phone requesting an ambulance. I run to his side and get down on my knees next to him. I look to Luca since he has gone through some medical training. "Tell me what to do."

Luca strips his jacket and rolls his sleeves up to his elbows. I follow his lead and do the same. Luca puts his hand under his nose and I see some of the tension leave his body. "He's breathing." I feel my shoulders slightly relax. He checks his pulse next. Luca looks over at me. "It's weak. Help me turn him on his left side." He points at a waitress standing over us. "You. Get some aspirin. There should be some in the first aid kit."

I look at her over my shoulder as we begin turning my dad to his side. "The kit is in my office in my top right desk drawer." I hear her footsteps as she walks away.

I feel myself going numb as I see blood start to pool under his head. It feels like it takes the waitress an eternity to return with the aspirin, and even longer for the ambulance to arrive. I step out of the way as the paramedics swarm my dad with machines I hope I never have to see again.

They are all talking so fast it is like a low hum in the distance. Luca is suddenly in my face, both hands on my shoulders. "He's going to be okay. I'll take care of things here. Go with him. I'll drive Rosalie and Juli. We'll be right behind you."

Rosa. Where is Rosa? My vision clears, my eyes having trouble focusing. I see the paramedics wheeling my father out the door of the kitchen. I follow after them. There's no sign of Rosa or Juli in the main room. I just hope like hell my dad is going to be okay.

34

LISTEN CLOSELY

Rosalie

MY HEART SINKS AS I watch Matteo run back through the doors. Juli stands and puts her hand over her mouth. "Oh my god. He has to be okay."

Her voice is like a low roar in my ears. I feel light headed. Memories of that day crashing back into me. Crying while the paramedics held me. Asking everyone around me over and over again where my dad was. Watching as they drug his lifeless body from the water's edge. The social worker trying to shield me from the horrible sight that will forever be ingrained in my mind.

I'm suddenly being shaken, a small voice growing louder and louder. "Rosalie! Rosalie!"

I shake my head as if I can clear my mind of all those memories. I blink a few times to clear my vision. I look around me. I'm sitting on the ground on the side of the parking lot of Moretti's. Juli is kneeling down in front of me, worry etched on her face. I run my hand along the rough pavement, the gravel leaving scuff marks on my hands.

The last few moments suddenly crash back into me. "Lorenzo." I should never have gotten attached. I should have never opened myself up to this pain again.

Luca appears from around the corner. "Thank fuck I found you two. I've been looking all over. We need to get going. The traffic will be horrible this time of night." He looks down at me. "What happened? Are you alright?" He looks over to Juli. "Is she alright?"

"I'm fine." I call on all my strength to push myself up off the ground. I sway for a moment before I regain my balance. Luca and Juli exchange a look of concern before Juli grabs my arm and leads me to Luca's car.

I sit in the front seat and glare out the side window for the entire forty-five minute drive. I am barely holding myself together. My thoughts bounce back and forth between wanting to be there for Matteo and trying to keep the memories at bay.

When we finally pull into the hospital we are all on edge. We haven't heard from Matteo since he left in the ambulance. I can see Alda's car a few cars down. I'm glad she'll be able to be here for Matteo.

Luca parks and the two of them rush out of the car. I open my door, but as soon as my feet hit the ground I sink down to my knees and sob.

Juli kneels down in front of me, compassion all over her face. In between sobs I manage to say, "I can't watch him lose his dad. I'm not strong enough."

Juli looks up at Luca, "Go on. We will be right behind you." I hear him run toward the emergency room door. Juli sits next to me and leans back against the side of the car and gently rubs my back as I sob.

Matteo

I'm sitting on the floor somewhere in the hospital. I couldn't even tell you what floor I'm on, only that my dad disappeared through those doors almost an hour ago. I've been sitting here ever since. They took him straight to surgery after we arrived.

I've never been so scared. When I sat and watched my mom OD, I didn't even cry. That sounds awful, but it's the truth. I sat there and watched her pass out before I called 911.

This feeling of hopelessness is gutting me. I lean my head back against the wall and look up at the ceiling once again. I wish Rosa was here. As much as I hate how dependent I have gotten on her. I guess I should get used to taking care of myself again.

I hear frantic footsteps coming around the corner. I jump up expecting to find a nurse coming with an update. Instead I'm met with Luca running down the hallway. He sighs when he sees me. "Thank fuck. I've been searching for almost 20 minutes. Didn't you get my calls?"

I shake my head. "No cell signal."

He puts his hands on his hips. "Shit. Have you heard anything?"

I shake my head once again. "No. Hopefully soon. The doctors said it should take thirty minutes to an hour. Where is Rosa?"

"She's downstairs. I found Alda in a waiting room downstairs. I told her to stay put until I could find you."

The double doors open and a nurse walks through. "Matteo?"

I turn and raise my hand. "I'm here. How is he?"

"I'm the nurse that's been assigned to your father's case. Follow me this way."

Luca moves to follow us, but the nurse stops him. "Only one family member. Sorry."

Luca pats me on the back. "I'll be here if you need me."

I nod as I follow the nurse through the doors. "Your father just got out of surgery. We only had to put one stent in, so that's good news. He's in recovery now. He was already starting to wake up when I left." She looks at me and smiles. "He's going to be okay."

I feel tears form at the immense relief I feel. I follow her through the halls until we reach the recovery unit. We finally make it to my dad's room. She opens the door and I see him sitting up in the bed. A smile takes over my face when I see him trying to work the remote.

When he sees me, he smiles. "Ah! You're here. You don't happen to have my glasses do you? I can't see these darn buttons."

The nurse laughs. "I see someone is feeling better." She looks over at me. "I'll leave you two alone. He should rest tonight. The doctor will be by to talk to you in the morning. You can stay as long as you'd like."

She closes the door and I go over to sit on the edge of the bed. My dad is still examining the buttons on the remote. I reach out and gently grab the remote so I can lay it on the bed. "How are you, dad?"

I can tell he is tired, but other than that he looks pretty good. He yawns. "I'm just tired." He pats me on the arm. "No need to fuss. I'm going to be just fine. I had to get a few stitches on my head. Apparently when I fell, I hit my head on the counter. I've got a pretty big knot to show for it too."

I reach out and grab his hand. "You scared us half to death, dad."

He smiles at me. "Scared me pretty bad too. I'm glad things weren't too bad." He looks around the room. "Where is Rosalie?"

I stand and move a chair next to his bed so I'm not crowding him. "She's downstairs." I glance down at my lap. "She's leaving, dad. They always leave."

He tilts his head to the side. "Why?"

I sit down in the seat and lean back, thankful for a softer place to sit than the floor. "She got the job."

He scratches his chin. "So she accepted?"

I shrug. "Seemed like she was excited about it to me."

"Have you asked her to stay?"

I shake my head as I cross my arms across my chest. "No. I didn't want to influence her decision."

"Do you want her to stay?"

I throw my hands in the air. "Of course I do." He tries to lean forward, but gets snagged on some wires. I hold my hands out in front of me. "Don't push it."

He motions for me to come closer. "Well you come here then." I do as he says. "Listen closely. That girl is special." I open my mouth, but he holds up his hand to stop me. "Listen to everything I have to say. After everything that girl went through with her dad, she still showed up here for you. You're a fool if you think that girl is going anywhere. You go down there and beg her to stay here with you. You fight for her to stay or you'll spend the rest of your life wondering what if."

I lean forward, "But—"

He holds his hand out to silence me once more. "No buts. I see what she has done for you. You'll regret it for the rest of your life if you don't do everything in your power to keep her."

"I can't just leave you here like this."

He wags his finger at me. "Like hell you can't. Get out of here. Come back and tell me all about it in the morning."

I stand and kiss my dad on the forehead and say, "I'll see you in the morning." I turn and run out the door.

I barely hear him say, "You better bring Rosalie with you! And my glasses!"

I run down the halls, trying to find my way out of this maze. A few nurses yell at me to stop running, but I don't give a damn. I feel like I'm running in circles until I hear a clicking sound. I stop in my tracks. I know that sound. I round a corner and come face to face with Rosa. She's pacing back and forth down a hallway. Her phone screen lights up her face. Her shoes are making the familiar click on the tile floor.

She looks up from her phone screen and starts running. I open my arms and let her warmth consume me. Frosting and sunshine filling my nose. Home. This is home.

I can feel her tears run down my neck where she buries her face. "I'm so sorry! How is he? Can we go see him?"

I run my hand down the back of her head as she pulls back to look me in the eye. Her big brown eyes staring back at me. "Stay with me."

She nods her head. "I'm here. Whatever you need."

I shake my head. "No. Not here at the hospital. Here, in Italy. Stay with me. You asked me once if I had one day left to live, how would I spend it. I would spend it with you. You're my true north, Rosa." I kiss her cheek. "Let me show you every day how I would spend my last day." Then I kiss her nose. "Stay with me." Then I kiss her lips. "I love you, Rosa."

She smiles at me, I've never seen such a beautiful sight. "I was never going anywhere." She pulls me in for a kiss that almost makes me fall to my knees. "I love you too, Matteo."

I feel my phone vibrate in my pocket. It doesn't let up as I kiss her. When we finally pull away I pull my phone out of my pocket while I hold Rosa with my other hand. "What the hell?"

She laughs, "That was probably me."

I go to unlock my phone but she pushes my phone away. I smile at her. "Hey! I want to read them!"

She shakes her head. "There isn't anything on there that hasn't already been said." She pulls me down for another kiss, and all is right in the world.

Can you die from happiness? I guess I'll find out for all of us.

35

HOME

Rosalie

I PUSH THE DOOR open and set the duffel bag on the floor. I turn in time to see Lorenzo shooing Matteo away as he gets out of the car. "I don't need help. I'm fine. Stop your fussing."

Matteo holds his hands up in surrender as Alda gets out of her car parked just behind Lorenzo's. "If you want something to do, help me carry in these groceries."

Matteo just laughs as he goes over to help his aunt carry in a vast amount of groceries she insisted Lorenzo needed. Lorenzo walks through the door and pats me on the shoulder. "I told them not to worry about me. I'll be just fine. There's really no need to fuss."

I smile as he walks by. "We all deserve to be taken care of every now and then." I pick up his duffle bag. "Where do you want this?"

He motions down a long hallway to my left as he walks into the living room. "Second door on the right. You can just set it on the bed. I'll take care of it later."

I make my way down the long hallway, stopping every few feet to admire the family photos on the walls. My favorite is the one of Matteo climbing a natural rock wall with a huge smile on his face. He's probably around 16 years old. His knees are scraped up and his hair is a mess from being outside all day, but he looks so happy.

When I open Lorenzo's bedroom door I find a queen size bed, a small night stand, and a dresser covered in more photos.

I turn when I hear footsteps behind me. I can't help but smile when I see Matteo come around the corner. He returns my smile ten-fold. "Alda was wondering if you wanted to help with dinner while I help dad get settled."

I walk into his open arms. "I would love to."

He pulls my face back and rubs his thumb across my cheek. I lean into his touch while he searches my face. He must find what he's looking for because he says, "Open a restaurant with me." He must see the confusion on my face, because his smile only grows. "I've been thinking about what I want ever since my dad's heart attack. This is what I want, Rosa. Owning a restaurant with you. Working with you everyday like we have been doing for the past few weeks. You can do all our marketing and even take on other clients if you want to. We can even travel around Europe and you can continue your blog. What do you think?"

A smile takes over my face. "I think it sounds perfect." He pulls me in for a mouth watering kiss that takes my breath away. Home. I'm finally home.

One Year Later

Rosalie

THE BELL RINGS SIGNALING an order is ready. I'm sitting at our private booth in the back working on my next blog post. This has been one of the busiest days we've had since opening a few months ago.

The bell rings again. I get up and smooth out my sundress. The waiters could probably use some help. When I step into the kitchen I catch Matteo's eye. He's sporting a dish rag draped over shoulder, his shirt sleeves rolled up past his elbows, and a smile that lights up my world.

He never looks away as I walk over to his station. He wipes his hands on the dish rag and pulls me in for a kiss that I feel all the way to my toes. The room is suddenly filled with noise. Our sous chef shouts, "Get a room!" A few others whistle, while the rest say in unison, "Aww!"

The bell digs again and I pull away from the kiss with a smile on my face. Matteo gives me a little tap on the butt as I walk away. "Come find me later."

I wink at him over my shoulder. "You can count on it." Laughter erupts from the stations closest to Matteo.

I put the dishes on a serving tray and look at the ticket to see what table I need to go to. I get excited when I see it's a table outside. I could use some fresh air. Maybe I'll walk across the street to see Juli when I get done.

I lean back against the front door to push it open since my hands are full. I start making my way to the furthest table from the door. I can see an older man sitting with his back to me. He has his cane propped against the side of the building. Even from behind I can tell he is wearing a flat cap and a tan suit.

"Hello, sir. Sorry about your wait. I have your order right here." He looks up at me and I can finally see his face. "Gus?" I didn't mean to say that out loud. I'm sure he thinks I'm a crazy person.

"Salvestro. It's nice to see you again. I see The Eden Valley stole your heart just like so many others."

I put his food down on the table and put the tray under my arm. "More like I gave my heart away."

He motions to the other seat in front of him. "Would you like to sit with me?"

I pull out the chair and sit down. "Are you here visiting your family?"

He nods his head as he situates his napkin in his lap. "I am. I have a new grandson." I smile as he shows me photos of his growing family.

I can't keep the smile off my face. I never thought I would get to see him again. "Do you remember what you said to me that day outside of the train station?"

He takes a sip of coffee before he answers. "I don't recall anything in particular."

"You said, 'Our hearts are like a compass. They have a way of pointing us in the right direction. When you feel that pull, you'll know what you should do.'"

"Sounds like good advice."

I nod my head and look down at the ring on my left ring finger and smile. "It really was." A group of businessmen walk through the door. "I better go. The lunch rush is about to start. It was so good to see you again. Make sure to come by next time you're in the area."

He smiles and tips his hat. "Thank you for sitting with me today."

I wipe my hands on my apron and walk through the front door. "Welcome to Bella Rosa. Booth or table?"

The End

Stracciatella Gelato

Serves 6
500ml Fresh Cream
4 Egg Yolks
100gr Dark Chocolate, Chopped
80gr Granulated Sugar

1. In another bowl and using an electric whisk, cream the egg yolks and sugar together until the sugar granules have dissolved and the mixture has turned a pale yellow color.

2. Fold in the chopped chocolate into the egg yolk mixture.

3. Whip the cream.

4. Fold the whipped cream into the chocolate and egg yolk mixture.

5. Place on a tray and freeze for 8 hours.

Tiramisu

Serves 6

4 Egg Yolk

180g Sugar

180g Fresh Cream (Heavy Cream)

2 Cups Fresh Black Coffee

Lady Fingers (Savoiardi or Pavesini)

1. Beat the egg yolk and sugar until they are double the size.

2. Whisk in the mascarpone until combined.

3. Whisk the cream in a separate bowl. Then fold into the mascarpone egg mixture.

4. Spoon some mascarpone mixture into the bottom of the jar. Now add a layer of coffee soaked lady fingers. Dust each layer with cocoa powder for a rich flavor.

About the Author

Katie B. Wright is a contemporary romance author who lives in Tennessee. When she's not writing, she loves checking off books from her mile long TBR list, gaming, and spending time with her husband.

KatieBWright.com

Find Katie on social media @KatieBWrightAuthor